RANCHER IN TRAINING

PART-TIME COWBOYS, BOOK 1

MARIE JOHNSTON

LE PUBLISHING

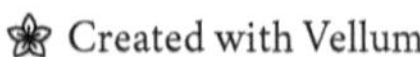 Created with Vellum

For my Family. You're worth it.

For all the latest news, sneak peeks, quarterly short stories, and free material sign up for my newsletter.

Deputy Farah James arrests bad boys, she doesn't date them. So when an ex-con with a fiery past returns to town, she ignores the criminal things he does to her pulse. Behind bars, Jesse Rodriguez and his wicked looks were easy to dismiss, but as a free man with a life to reclaim, he's never been more dangerous to her—or her job and the ranch that depends on her paycheck.

When stopping to help a stranded motorist puts Jesse on the radar of the local deputy, for once, he doesn't complain. After all, Farah's just as cute as he remembers. Too bad she's also an icy professional who doubts he's a changed man. He's willing to give her up as a lost cause and make his way out of town—until an accident strands him at the ranch next door.

Crossing paths on duty is one thing, but seeing how good Jesse is with his hands threatens everything she's ever worked for. But Farah's not the only one taking a risk, and he refuses to torch his future again, even if it means leaving her in his rearview mirror for good.

CHAPTER 1

*D*on't stop. It'll only lead to trouble. Don't stop.

He was almost out of the county, on his way to… Home wasn't the right word. The roof he was staying under for the next several nights.

Damn. Jesse let off the gas. Ahead, an old pickup was stalled on the side of the road, the hood up but no smoke tendrils curled from the engine. A good sign for the owner. With Jesse's background, the last thing he should do was walk up to a stranger and offer to help. People didn't look at him and think *This is a good guy*, and given where he was geographically, they would probably shoot him for his efforts.

But an engine in trouble was like a siren song, and he no longer took for granted working on one.

Idling to a stop, he killed the engine, hoping it'd convince whoever was under the hood that he wasn't going to attack or abduct them, that his intentions were only to have a look-see at the engine and offer his expert advice.

And he wasn't being arrogant. There wasn't a set of pistons he couldn't coax into thrusting again, and he had tools in the back of his own beat-up truck. He'd spent the weekend with his sister and her new husband, who thankfully didn't have it in his genetics to carry a grudge for what Jesse had done to the family. Jesse and Josie had wasted hours in the shop doing some light bodywork on an old Charger she was restoring.

How's Brock handling it not being a Mustang? he'd asked.

It's my project. Then she'd grinned because it wouldn't matter to her husband if she'd brought back a Volvo to redo. Jesse's brotherly heart had damn near combusted like gasoline under pressure. Much like her spouse, Jesse would do anything for her, but he had a long way to come up in her estimation. His only solace was that suffering through his fuckup had brought her true love and gotten her out from under the manipulative thumb of her father.

He and Josie shared a mother, but her dad certainly hadn't been his.

Although, if he had been, Jesse wouldn't have epically upended his life for an impossible fantasy.

On that happy thought, he got out. It was just him and the other pickup on the quiet county road. They were surrounded by fence posts, barbed wire, and black fields that would soon be turning green with whatever crop had been planted last month. The warm mid-May sun shone down on the land, but a cool spring breeze wafted over him. The repressed city kid in him reveled in all nature had to offer.

At the sound of his door shutting, a head popped out next to the open hood.

Relief coursed through Jesse like a power sprayer. The stranded motorist was a man. If it'd been a chick and he'd scared her, he would've been the subject of a 9-1-1 call. He was the stranger in a land of good ol' boys, and it wouldn't matter that his sister had married into the most influential family in the county; Jesse would be guilty by default.

Three of his four grandparents had emigrated from Mexico. He'd been born and raised in Minnesota, like his parents, but with his ink-black hair and brown skin, people often asked if he spoke English. Residents in Moore would assume he was a migrant worker and be suspicious, or worse, recognize him and call the cops.

At the thought of law enforcement, a vision of hard green eyes and a pert little body flashed through his mind. He should've forgotten *her* by now. Just thinking about her meant his common sense still hadn't risen to a safe level.

"Hey," the guy called, yanking Jesse away from useless thoughts. Apparently, he wasn't fazed by Jesse's presence. This day might not suck.

"Do you know what's making her complain?" Jesse tugged on the greasy rag hanging from his pocket thanks to a last-minute touchup on Josie's Charger before he'd left. He wouldn't bother with his tool kit until he knew what was wrong, but maybe he should grab it. Being a mechanic was as much a part of him as his black hair and brown eyes, but people looked at him and his arms filled with tattoos and thought thug or gangster. But his oil-smudged jeans and grungy shirt should scream grease-head more than homeless.

Which he wasn't. He just hadn't committed to an address yet.

"I'm afraid I don't speak old-ass truck." The guy stepped around the hood.

Jesse's brows popped at the badge on the guy's chest. For fuck's sake. And he'd thought this day wouldn't suck like so many others.

Wait, just a fireman. It could be worse.

He could've been a cop.

Jesse forced a grin. "Old-ass truck is one of the easiest languages to learn when it comes to engines. Mind if I take a look?"

The fireman stepped aside. Jesse circled around and peered at the hunk of metal under the hood, trying not to be intimidated by the uniform. This guy wasn't a cop, but his crisp navy-blue shirt with its yellow-and-red badge on the chest was enough to kick Jesse's heart rate up.

Putting his hands on the warm edge of the old Chevy's frame, he squinted at the engine. "Did it make any noise before it died?"

The fireman snorted. "It made an ungodly amount of noise, but nothing unusual. It just quit. Shut the hell down on me."

There were plenty of issues under the hood, but this problem was easy enough. "It's your battery. I could try to jump it, but the battery looks older than either of us and badly corroded. I can't believe it started in the first place."

The fireman went to shove a hand through his short, styled hair but stopped and glanced at his dusty palms. Dropping his hands, he glared at the vehicle. "Actually, I had to jump it before I left. It's been sitting on my land for a while and I wanted to get it—and keep it—running."

Jesse made the offer before he could think about what an abysmal idea it was to go into Moore's city limits. "I can give you a ride to pick a new one up and bring you back."

The fireman's brows jumped. "Seriously? Thanks, but—" He looked at his bulky black watch and winced. "I've gotta start my shift in five minutes."

Don't do it. Don't make the offer.

Jesse's newfound mission to *Be Better* couldn't be silenced. Probably because it had help from *I'm So Fucking Bored*. He'd left his recent job after only a few months when he'd caught a whiff of shady car sales. That situation was a big nope, and he'd blown that used-car lot and fix-it garage so fast he'd left skid marks.

Not going back to his old life. Not for anyone, starting with an idiot of a greedy boss.

Josie was helping him out, but he'd been resolved to turn his life around long before his little vacay at her place. When he'd learned he had a little niece or nephew coming, there was no choice. He could only make Josie proud.

The words left his mouth and he couldn't take them back. "I can give you a ride and grab a battery. If you wanna give me the key, I'll come back, install the battery, and leave the key in the truck."

The man eyed him. "Seriously? Are you like my fairy god-bro in denim?"

A chuckle burst from him. "Yeah, man. That's me to a T." He eyed the engine. "No, I was on my way out of town, but rehabbing engines is my profession. I've got nothing else going on. But…you're buying the battery."

"I'm paying you for the work, too. At least once I have proof that you didn't steal this beast and sell it on the black market for all the five hundred dollars you might get for it."

"Five hundred? You're an optimistic one."

The man grinned. He was likely five or so years younger than Jesse's own thirty-three. He stuck his hand out. "The name's Caleb Cruise. If it's not obvious, I need a ride to the firehouse."

"Jesse." *Please don't ask for a last name.* He shook Caleb's hand, then dropped it with a sigh. He glanced out at the flat field. No way was he giving his full name.

JESSE TURNED onto the highway that'd lead him straight into Moore. Caleb lived on the opposite side of the highway than Josie and Brock and the rest of the Walkers. Jesse had been taking the back roads out of town because he was in no hurry to return.

And he loved the country. Nothing was more beautiful than Minnesota in summer. It might be a winter wasteland the rest of the year, but these flowers and trees in bloom made everything worth it. Maybe it was his dormant farmer genes coming to life. This land was in his blood. Nothing else could explain the rage he'd felt when he'd learned his family's legacy had been stolen from him while he toiled away under a worthless excuse for a man who'd planned to screw him out of everything he'd worked for.

But enough of living in the past. He couldn't afford to let it affect his future more than it had. Josie was expecting her first kid and dammit, he wasn't going to be the absent uncle.

They passed farm-implement dealers, a vet clinic, and a car lot on the outskirts of town. Caleb seemed nice enough, but Jesse would be glad when his good deed was done and he was on his way back to St. Cloud.

Caleb drummed his fingers against the door. "What brings you to Moore?"

"I was visiting family and taking the back roads home."

Caleb raised a brow. "Why? Expired tabs?"

"Enjoying the view," he said, trying to act relaxed. "Not hiding from the cops." Not really.

"Don't take it personally. You don't look like a long-walks-in-the-park guy."

Jesse glanced down at the arm with the tribal tattoo. He wished it meant something, but he'd just seen it, liked it, had it done. Being eighteen and cocky was the real reason for the ink. He looked back at Caleb with his shaved sides, the hair on top longer and easy to style a little punk if he was off duty. His ear lobe was slightly elongated, like it was missing a small-caliber plug, and if Jesse were to peer closer, the guy's eyebrow had probably been pierced at one time.

"No offense, but you don't look like a guy living off the land."

Instead of a quick grin, Caleb's features tightened. "It's a new development."

"Oh yeah?" he asked mostly to keep the topic off himself.

"Yep. Forty acres, surrounded by two quarters of land and eighty head of cattle. More than enough for little old me." He jutted his chin up. "Take the left up here. The firehouse is on the block east of that stone monstrosity."

The building he gestured to was the courthouse. A block east meant Jesse wouldn't have to get up close and personal with the imposing building.

He followed the directions, then parked in front of the three-story brick firehouse. Two large garage doors let out on the back of the building, and American and Minnesota state flags flew on metal poles posted in the lawn by the sidewalk. Jesse's hands shook. He fisted them around the steering wheel to keep Caleb from noticing.

He was a convicted arsonist sitting outside a firehouse. Part of him expected to hear the wails of a police car behind him.

Caleb tossed his pickup key in the cup holder and pulled out his wallet. "How much is a battery?"

"Depends how good of one you want."

"Cheap as hell."

"Seventy-five dollars should be good."

Digging several twenties out, he tossed them down with the key. "When you're done, just hide the key under the front seat and don't lock the door. I'll get a ride back in the morning when my shift is done."

"No problem." He planned to also leave the extra money under the seat. Sure, he could use the income, but it didn't feel like help if he took money. He was turning over a new engine, as it were.

"Seriously, thanks man. Call the firehouse and ask for me if there's any trouble." He jumped out and trotted to the entrance. When he disappeared, Jesse didn't linger. He kept his truck at the speed limit all the way out of downtown, but the effort was exhausting. No more trouble, and he'd watched enough movies to know that it was when a guy thought things were picking up that his life always nose-dived.

He stopped at the auto-parts store. They should have a battery and fewer people than the super-sized department store in town. Grabbing his ball cap from the bench seat in the back of the cab, he tucked it low on his head. It was a shitty disguise, but maybe it'd get him in and out of the store without suspicion.

He strode in, Caleb's cash in hand. Selecting the lowest-end battery like Caleb had asked, he carried it to the cash register. Thankfully no one was in line.

Keeping his head down, he paid, passed on his thanks without meeting the man's eyes, and strode out. He breathed a sigh of relief as he crawled back into his truck. Getting out of Moore might just go smoothly.

Back at Caleb's truck, Jesse parked and grabbed an adjustable wrench to change the batteries. He carried the new one over, opened the hood up, and went about removing and brushing off the corroded posts.

The breeze kept him cool while the sun beat down on his back. A guy could get used to this. Even this simple act was a Zen moment. He didn't know if it was working outside or having his hands busy in an engine again that did it.

An engine approached. He planned to ignore it—until it slowed down. Fuck. Why couldn't he be the only Good Samaritan on the road today? He straightened and nailed his head on the hood, knocking his cap from his head. It tumbled to the ground as he swore and rubbed the back of his head.

As he bent to pick up the cap, he caught sight of the car that had stopped.

A patrol car.

Aw, hell. He was buried in a vehicle that didn't belong to him and he wasn't from around here, but that was the least of his troubles. His heart hammered as he stepped to the side, bringing him into the driving lane. He raised his hands out to the side and squinted at the cop car.

He was in the county, so it was either the sheriff or a deputy who'd stopped. The light bar was flashing, but its brightness was lost in the vibrant day.

The door opened. He mentally practiced his explanation. Stuttering over his story wouldn't help him.

Someone was getting out. The glimpse of flaxen hair underneath the brown hat almost stopped his heart.

No. It couldn't be. Didn't she work at the jail?

She had to clear the door for him to get a good view of her petite frame. The weapons belt clung to her hips like he'd dreamed of doing, only he'd hug them better than the bulky belt. A tactical vest, probably bulletproof, covered her torso, and his first thought was that it wasn't enough to protect her, even though it swamped her delicate body. Cop gear must not be made for the feminine body. And he'd rather see her in head-to-toe body armor.

Farah James's steely gaze punched into him, then widened.

"When'd they let you out of the jail?" he asked, missing the irony before he said the words.

Her gaze narrowed, her pink lips pursing. "When'd they let you out of prison, Jesse Rodriguez?"

CHAPTER 2

hat the ever-loving hell was he doing here?

The man was a criminal. A sinfully rugged felon with an intense gaze that could just as well strip her clothes off, tattoos that could theoretically be traced with a tongue—not her own, of course—and a body built by Craftsman.

He was the most dangerous thing in her line of work. If she crashed her car while in pursuit or got shot in a standoff, at least she'd go down on the job. But this guy could ruin her career if she so much as blushed at his attention.

Oh, she knew he found her attractive. Most guys around here knew to stay away from her. As the former sheriff's daughter, she hadn't been a highly sought-after date. Things hadn't changed now that she was twenty-six and a deputy.

She'd worked her ass off to get taken seriously and away from jail duty.

Jesse Rodriguez and his intense eyes and hard body weren't going to mess it up.

The corner of his mouth lifted. He was good at that, too. A half smile. Mysterious. Sexy. Inviting. Lethal was what it was. She knew what he'd done and yet a very girly part of her wanted to explain away the bad-boy behavior, climb onto his lap, and tell him all was forgiven.

She refused to be that girl, the one who lost her common sense over flexing biceps. Even if Jesse had an admirable set.

This was the job she'd worked her ass off for despite the snorts of disbelief. Since her first memory of seeing her mom walk through the door, decked out in all her gear, this was the only career Farah had wanted. Too bad she hadn't gotten her mom's height and intimidating glare.

"I did my time. I'm a free man." His hands lowered, and while he wasn't wearing a shit-eating grin, it was in the crinkles at the corners of his eyes. When he'd been jailed in Moore, he'd never smiled. Always angry. Except for when he was around her. Only then had his personal rage dimmed, but he was still intense. And when that intensity was focused on her, it was powerful enough to kick doors down.

"What about probation?"

He'd gotten five years for burning down Dillon Walker's shop and ruining the equipment inside. She'd heard Dillon hadn't been a random target. His land had been in Jesse's family generations ago. If Dillon's grandma hadn't kept it after being widowed, it would've been passed down to Jesse by his own grandma.

What had made him take up the grudge so many years later? And did it have anything to do with why he was here now?

She kept her hands planted on her hips, unable to summon any concern that he was a physical threat to her— beyond the unwanted yearning he inspired.

"Done. Like I said, free man."

Had five years gone by that quickly?

She glanced from him to the pickup he'd been...what?

Working on? The temperature dropped a good five degrees just from taking her eyes off him.

Wait. That was Caleb's truck. She hadn't seen him drive it since high school, but she'd know it anywhere. A second beater of a truck was parked behind it. That must be Jesse's. She had scanned the situation as she'd pulled up, but she took a closer look now.

Jesse was a convicted felon. He'd vandalized equipment and set property on fire. What was he doing with Caleb's truck?

"What's going on here?" she asked in what Dad joked was her cop voice.

A muscle jumped in his jaw before he answered, "I'm changing a battery."

She gave him a flat stare. He had to know that she'd be suspicious of his intentions. What he might not know is how good of friends she was with Caleb.

Jesse didn't waver under her perusal. He looked like he'd strolled right out of a mechanic's shop garage door, so different was he without the orange jumpsuit of the jail. His navy-blue-and-white cap had lost its whiteness long ago. Same with his shirt. But instead of turning her off, the shirt showed his muscles to rippling perfection when he moved. Same with his jeans. Snug around his waist and the tops of his thighs before draping down his frame like they were tailored to him. He wore athletic shoes that were in good shape but as scuffed and dirty as the rest of him. Except he wasn't dirty.

Unless she counted the look in his eye that promised to make her beg for dirty, wicked things. Not *her* per se. But a girl. Any girl. Just not her. She was too smart to fall for any of that.

Just like she was too savvy to get derailed in her questioning. "A battery? Does Caleb know that?"

She expected the anger that flashed in his eyes, but not the other emotions it was mixed with. Hurt. Regret. Defeat.

What had prison been like for him? It didn't often change people for the better and she should remember that. Jesse wouldn't be the same guy that had lingered in Moore's jail for months.

"Yes, he knows," Jesse said tightly. "I stopped to help him. He had to get to work and I offered to fix it and leave the key in the vehicle when I'm done."

"Why would you do that?" It was her job to ask, but she couldn't help hanging on his answer.

"Because I'm a nice guy."

She lifted a brow. His tone was sarcastic, but defensive. She could almost believe that he wasn't trying to steal Caleb's truck, though the damn thing would cost more money to hock than it'd return.

Jesse shrugged. "Give him a call and check with him yourself."

"Sure." She tilted her head. "What's his number?"

"I don't have it."

"Why would he turn over the keys and not give you his phone number?" Caleb *would* actually do that, but he had to know who Jesse was. The guy was best friends with one of the Walkers. Unless Jesse hadn't been completely truthful about his identity.

"Cuz he said to call the firehouse and ask for him if I had any issues. I have an issue." At Jesse's pointed look, she stamped down disappointment. Well, she'd been called worse.

She jutted her chin to the road in front of the open hood. "Stand over there while I call."

His expression said *seriously?* but his lips were clamped together. Spinning on one foot, he stomped to where she'd gestured.

Her belly fluttered. The swagger. His ass. If he hadn't had that firm butt on his first day of jail—not that she'd noticed—she'd wonder if he'd done nothing in prison but pump iron.

Stopping on the white line of the driving lane, he propped his hands on his hips and stared at her.

She kept him in the corner of her eye as she crossed to the pickup and looked at the engine. It appeared as if his story was true. An adjustable wrench rested on top of an old corroded battery, and a new one waiting to be installed was sitting on the pavement in front of the fender.

Jesse's sister was married to a Walker. Farah wasn't surprised Jesse had visited her—well, maybe a little, but Brock had helped Josie leave a toxic situation. Jesse probably didn't a hold a grudge against him and Brock wasn't like the rest of his cousins. He probably didn't care that Jesse was part of Josie's life, despite his history.

But that didn't explain why Jesse had run across Caleb. "What were you doing in this part of the county?"

"Driving through Moore isn't exactly the best thing for me to do, is it?"

She didn't miss the shame that flashed through his light-brown eyes. They were a few shades darker than her shirt, falling between her taupe uniform top and her chocolate-brown pants. His naturally bronzed skin nearly glittered under the spring sun, only making his shirt deadlier with how it enclosed his hard body.

To keep her gaze from lingering inappropriately on his body, she pulled out her phone. Caleb answered after a ring. "Hey. It's me."

Jesse's eyes narrowed. Did he not like how familiar she was with Caleb, or had it taken him by surprise? His stillness was like a predator who wasn't sure what prey he'd stumbled upon.

"'Sup, James?"

She finished her explanation. "I've got a man here who says he's changing a battery for you."

"Jesse, right? Yeah, he's cool. You and I both know that truck isn't getting stolen by anyone."

Her lips curved. The old Chevy was silver and orange, but the orange was scratched and faded so badly that those who hadn't grown up with Caleb wouldn't guess its original shade. If it hadn't been parked for the last decade since Caleb's grandpa passed away, it'd still be a good truck. Her smile died as she glanced at Jesse. His shoulders were rigid, and all his tension resided in his flattened mouth.

She met Jesse's gaze as she spoke into the phone. "Did he happen to tell you his last name when he agreed to help you?" Should she have gone there? Caleb had entrusted his property to a stranger. Had said stranger been honest?

"Does it matter? I had to get to work." Caleb lowered his voice. "You know how the chief is."

She ground her teeth together. Yes, she did. Even worse, she knew how the chief's son was.

"Jesse Rodriguez." She waited for it to sink in but wasn't surprised when Caleb remained in his cloud of ignorance. It was his preferred state when bad stuff around him happened. "Remember the trouble the Walkers had?"

Jesse's gaze cut away to the empty field, his eyes full of shame. She had to look away, too, or she wouldn't be able to do her job. She was not a softy.

"Oh shit. Really? I didn't get that vibe from him."

"Well, just letting you know. Still okay with your arrangement?" If all was good between Jesse and Caleb, then her job here was done. So why was she searching for reasons to stick around?

"If he's really on the highway with a new battery, then yeah."

Sometimes she wished her outlook could be as hopeful as Caleb's.

"I'll hang around and make sure it ends well." She did not just say that. How could she even say it was her job? Jesse wasn't breaking the law.

But she had to log in the stop and by the time she was done, he'd be on his way in his own old truck.

"I owe you one, Farah." Caleb hung up.

No, he didn't. They never owed each other. The tally marks would be too many to count.

She tucked her phone away. Jesse was back to staring at her. An unwanted flush spread through her body. A breeze caressed her neck, sending shivers down her spine.

"Everything okay, Deputy?"

How ironic. It was difficult to get taken seriously as a law officer in the same town she'd grown up in. Everywhere she went, *Hey, Farah, how's your mom? Tell your dad I said hi.* Rarely was she addressed officially, not even by the sheriff who'd replaced her mother.

"Your story checks out. Caleb's okay with you finishing up here like planned."

"You two know each other?"

"It's Moore," she said flatly, mostly to keep from explaining herself, not at all because the hint of jealousy in his tone made the buried feminine side of her want to preen. But she couldn't help herself. "We're neighbors, and we went to school together."

Jesse looked around at the fields and tree rows forming the shelterbelts between them. In the distance, a cluster of trees protected Caleb's land, which he'd inherited from his grandparents. Hers was on the other side. She yanked her gaze away, not needing the stress that came with thinking of home.

He shook his head. "You two live out here?"

His surprise wasn't what she expected. "Did you think I'd have a condo in the city?"

"Does Moore even have condos?"

"Listen to you, city boy."

"Right. That's me." His smirk, though not quite a smile, transformed his face from hardened criminal to an appealing mechanic she could dream about. "No, I've been to Brock's. He and Josie spend like an entire day mowing the lawn. Nothing else. Just mowing. You and Caleb work and shit."

How had Jesse just summed up her entire stressful existence when he hardly knew her?

"It's not easy." If only the lawn was all she had to worry about. "I'm going to hang out until you're done." The lightness drained from his features and guilt speared her gut. "If I get another call, I'll have to leave." His wariness didn't fade and she elaborated despite her refusal to explain herself to anyone. "No one else will stop and bother you if they see me parked here."

Understanding lifted the shadows in his gaze. He dug out his wallet and withdrew his license. He handed it over.

This close, his scent lifted to her on the breeze. Was he wearing cologne or was that just fabric softener? His clothes were stained from work, though clean, but he could use oil for aftershave and she would still want to stop, drop, and roll in it.

"What's this for?" she asked. In her ear, the dispatcher, Evie, checked in. Farah pressed the button to the mic pinned on her collar. "Still at the scene."

"Don't you need my license and registration?"

"Did you do something wrong?" She handed it back.

"No?" He frowned down at the little card in his hand, his face shadowed by the brim of his hat. His shoulders were so wide. He was nothing but power and muscle. Her mouth went dry. Damn her self-imposed dating hiatus.

"The address on this is Moore," she said because she'd peeked at his details.

"It was easier to use Josie's place until I settle down."

"And you haven't yet."

He glanced away again. Once more, the flash of shame disappeared quickly. "No. I had four years of probation. I worked various jobs for two of them to save up for auto tech school the last two. After probation was over, I moved to St. Cloud. I thought I had a bead on a more permanent place, but the garage I was working for liked to deal drugs on the side. I left the guy I was renting a room from a couple months' worth of money and got the hell out of there."

Smart. He seemed like he was trying to change. She'd known people who'd tried but kept getting hit with shitty luck and couldn't move past it, devolving into their old ways. Would Jesse be another of those?

"Where are you staying now?"

He answered, probably because he thought she was asking as a cop and not as a Nosy Nellie. "I'm renting another room in St. Cloud. The other tenants are migrant field workers, so no lease."

"Got it."

He went back to the battery, and she went to work on her log. Taking her time, she was done almost when Jesse was. Had he been working slowly, too, or was it wishful thinking? And why would she hope for such a thing?

She climbed back out, grimacing at the way her belt cut into her hip. Another adjustment she'd have to make to her gear. The drone of an engine cut through the birds chirping in the nearby trees.

Her stomach fell when she recognized the hundred-thousand-dollar pickup that compensated for the fragile male ego behind its wheel. Chrome glinted in the sun with blinding showmanship. The driver had even put a lift kit on the truck so she'd need a rope ladder to climb into it. She'd never willingly get inside, but she'd impound it in a hot second.

Clinton Bradford. Fire Chief Bradford's son and her ex-boyfriend.

The engine rumbled louder as it approached. Jesse extracted himself from Caleb's pickup and sauntered to his own as he looked over his shoulder at the approaching obnoxious ride.

To her dismay, Clinton slowed to a stop in the middle of the quiet road and rolled his window down.

"Need a hand, Farah?" The way his gaze stroked her from head to toe sickened her.

"Everything's fine. Bye."

Jesse's head snapped to her, then back to Clinton. He didn't edge closer, but the initial tension from when she'd first stopped was back.

Clinton's hard blue gaze pinned Jesse, then lifted to the vehicles lined up behind him. "What's this guy doing with Caleb's truck?"

"You'll have to ask Caleb." Each time she was faced with Clinton Fucking Bradford, she couldn't believe she'd been so stupid at such a critical time in her life. This guy liked no one more than himself.

Clinton had the audacity to smile at her. "I'll do that, Ms. Farah."

"Deputy." He probably thought his banter was flirty and not hostile. "See you."

"Yeah, you will." He sped off, the rattle of whatever he did to his pipes momentarily deafening her.

Questions were lining up in Jesse's eyes, but he didn't ask. She wouldn't have told him if he had.

"Doesn't the county have a noise ordinance that includes his modified exhaust?"

"He keeps it legal." Barely. "You know where you're going to get back to St. Cloud?"

"I've made this trip before."

"All right." She couldn't bring herself to say goodbye. It'd come out too much like she'd said it to Clinton and Jesse hadn't earned that tone.

He started for his vehicle, but before he got in, she had to pass along a warning. "Jesse."

He paused in the open door, one hand on the frame. Another poster-worthy shot right there.

"Maybe...find another route next time. Clinton's gonna find out who you are and now he knows what you drive. He doesn't need a reason to be an asshole, and he doesn't miss one to act like it."

Jesse scanned around him again like he was seeing the sprouting soybean fields in a new light. "Got it. You ever get to mace him, I want to hear the story."

A laugh burst from her. "I'll save you the wait. Pepper spray. In the face. Two feet away."

Jesse grinned and it transformed his face. His eyes danced, and with the cap he looked like just another farm kid that had grown up around these parts. "I bet he deserved worse."

Her smile almost died, but she forced it to stay in place. "Yes, he did."

She must not have hidden the hurtful memories that bombarded her well enough. His expression grew serious. "What'd he do, Farah?"

He didn't use Deputy. She should be upset, but how he said her name made all the difference in the world. And no way was she sharing her personal humiliation. "Ever seen *Carrie?*"

"I read the book." Prowling closer, he reverted to the angry, dangerous man she'd met five years ago. "Is that what happened? He embarrassed you in front of an audience?"

"He tried to." And his audience had been what she dubbed the jack-off crew, with Clinton's brother the unwitting leader. But her mama hadn't raised a wilting flower. Farah was a cactus. Prickly and storing, she kept her emotions where no one could see them. "He thought he could dupe me, but I seasoned him pretty well."

"Did you use the whole can of Mace?"

"Pepper spray," she said automatically, the cop in her needing to make the distinction. Most sprays nowadays were pepper spray and no longer Mace, unless Jesse meant Mace Brand, but she doubted it. "I was pulled off him, but that was my intention."

"Good."

They fell silent. It would've been an easy break in conversation except she had a job to do and he should leave town before Clinton snooped into who she'd stopped by Caleb's truck. Somehow since the night of their "falling out," she'd morphed into the one that got away. The one he needed to conquer, probably for his pride.

She had to get going before she batted her eyes for the first time in her life. "Have a safe drive home." Touching the tip of her brim, she dipped her head. An old school move she'd picked up from Mom. *Keep the glint in your eye, and they'll take you seriously.* Today, she did it to keep professional distance between her and Jesse.

Had the last five minutes really happened? She'd joked around with Jesse Rodriguez, had sort of shared a part of her life.

Out of habit, Farah studied her surroundings. This was her home; she'd grown up riding horse through these lands. On the other side of the copse of trees, past Caleb's house and beyond hers, were her family's cattle.

If Clinton's parents didn't live so close to her place, she'd be suspicious about why he was lurking in the area. His property bordered the southern end of hers, but none of his pastures were nearby. The whole reason she'd been driving this way was to make sure her cattle were nice and cozy in the pasture.

She didn't want a repeat of last week when thirty head "found" a hole in the fence she'd just repaired.

She got into her patrol car and waited for Jesse to leave. He pulled away and stuck a hand out the window to wave.

The pang in her heart meant nothing as his vehicle faded into the distance. Unless he caused problems with the Walkers again, she knew what his truck looked like and could make sure not to cross paths with him again in the future.

CHAPTER 3

With the windows down, Jesse kept his arm resting out the window and the air flowing through his fingers. He'd even put his seat belt on to mollify Deputy James.

Farah.

Her name didn't suit her. When he'd first heard another officer call her by her first name, he'd almost choked. A boy's nickname, maybe. "Farah" summoned the woman from the show his stepdad had always watched. Feathered hair and tiny bikinis. But Deputy James bound her hair, and only the skin of her hands and face ever showed.

When in his life had he ever thought he would crush on a cop? She was cute. Her prickly demeanor made her even more enticing. Unlike some of her coworkers, she hadn't been a dick to any of the inmates. She'd treated them all professionally, coming down hard when some idiot got out of line but remaining fair and consistent the rest of the time. Other officers glared and snarled at him, but not her. He'd been nothing more than a job to her, and that was a step up from what he was used to.

Would he ever see her again? Just because she hadn't driven him out of town with orders to never show his face again didn't mean the rest of the town wouldn't do the job for her.

He'd stick to his routine. Come around for Josie, leave by the back roads.

He glanced around. This was where she was from?

The landscape was…calming. The fields would be green soon enough, turning to whatever color the crop was in the fall. Some would stay green, others would turn golden like wheat and barley, but his favorite was sunflowers. Not that he got to see them often. When he had deluded himself that Dillon Walker's property should rightfully be his, Jesse had fantasized about growing sunflowers.

Whatever. Stupid dream. What the hell did he know about farming? He didn't have land, he didn't have money, and he didn't have a bag of sunflower seeds in his truck.

He blew past his turn.

"Shit." He was tempted to stomp on the brakes, but there was no hurry. As long as he kept track of where he was going, he could backtrack his way out. His curiosity propelled him forward.

Just a little farther. Then he'd turn around and get back to St. Cloud.

Farah hadn't pointed out which farmhouse was hers. The ones out this way were older, the same with the barns and the shops. A few abandoned and dilapidated farmsteads were scattered around. Brown barns that had long ago lost their paint, sagging in the middle, half collapsed.

If he weren't a felon who'd already been approached by law enforcement, he'd search those areas just to see what was left behind.

But he might as well walk himself back to jail. The last

time he'd crept around someone's farmland, he'd lost his damn mind.

Still, he couldn't argue with the appeal of Moore, Minnesota. Too bad his grandma had moved all those years ago.

Too bad Dillon Walker's grandma hadn't given the land back to his family when her first husband, his great-uncle, had died.

Whatever.

He hit gravel and told himself one more mile, then he'd turn around. The window stayed open. A little dust never hurt him. He passed an approach to a cattle pasture. It'd be a good place to turnaround, but he'd get the next one.

An intersection came up. Gravel roads shot out in four directions. He turned right. He'd have to backtrack, but he could either retrace his route or take another right and head back to the highway.

To his left, black cattle roamed. To his right, a farmer was in a tractor on the far side of the field. Another right came up. Jesse took it. He had to get out of this county before he got himself in trouble.

Another pasture was on his left. Then a small, two-story white house. Even from this far away, he could tell it needed a paint job. The size of the property was admirable, though, and standard for this area. The same with the buildings. With his luck, this was Farah's place and he'd get caught.

Wait. How'd she ranch alone? With a full-time job?

Was she…married? She didn't wear a ring. In a relationship?

Farah would have to stay a mystery. Looking to his right, he eyed the tractor.

What a beast. What was it like to drive one of those? Get under the hood? Did they have a hood?

Guilt ate at him. He'd destroyed one of those. A nice piece of equipment, and sure, insurance had paid for it—

A flash of movement caught his attention. He was turning his head when the roar of an engine cut through the wind in his ears.

He yanked the wheel to the right as a black pickup hit the gravel, narrowly missing him. His own truck spun, its wheels catching the edge of the road where it dipped into the ditch. Then he was weightless as his pickup flipped.

JESSE'S TEMPLES POUNDED. His truck was quiet. After the shaking his ride had gotten, everything was shockingly quiet aside from the hissing under the hood.

Upside down. Jesse groaned and reached down—up?—his fingers searching for the buckle.

With one hand to brace himself, he unhooked himself and unceremoniously folded onto the roof, his head hitting first. Shimmying his way out, he met with a pair of boots. Squinting up, Jesse had to try three times before he straightened out his vision.

A man's voice intruded on his thoughts. "Yeah. By the Jameses north pasture. Hey, you okay?"

Jesse wanted to laugh, but his dizziness hadn't passed. "Yeah," he croaked and tried to stand. He plopped down on his knees. A few minutes sitting and he'd be fine.

"He's not okay, but he can talk," the guy said.

Was he the other driver?

No. No black pickup was in sight. Jesse scooted to the side to see past his pickup. The tractor he'd been admiring only minutes before was stopped in the field. The man on the phone must be the farmer. Was he on the phone with 9-1-1?

Jesse might want to see Farah again, but not like this. Not

when he'd crashed close to her property and looked guilty as fuck because the black truck had left him to die.

Sirens wailed in the distance. Jesse didn't bother looking over his shoulder. With this quick of a response, it was probably Farah.

The man continued talking on the phone. Jesse's heart sank when the guy said he hadn't seen the accident, just the overturned truck when he'd started another lap around the field.

Wasn't that fucking super.

Tires crunched, and Jesse spared the new arrival a glance. He didn't miss her gaze go from him to the pickup, and from worried to stone cold.

The farmer said, "Farah's here. I'll talk to her," and clipped his flip phone shut.

She got out. "Murphy. What's going on?" A bag was in her hand as she knelt by Jesse.

"This young man can't drive on gravel."

"I was trying to avoid an accident," Jesse growled.

"Your ABCs are obviously okay." Whatever those were. Farah squatted next to him and scanned his body like he was one of those crash-test dummies. Which was kind of what he felt like.

"No bleeding. Are you hurt anywhere?" She ducked her head to look into his eyes like she was trying to picture the accident through him.

"Just pissed." He propped his forehead in his hand. Could someone dim the sun for a few moments so he could collect his mental shit? "A black truck tore out of that pasture and almost T-boned me. Then the asshole didn't even stick around."

Suspicion flickered in her eyes. This close, the yellow ring around her pupils was stark against the green of her irises. She pointed to the approach that led to an old trail between the pasture and the field next to it. "The truck came from there? Did you see who was driving?"

"I didn't see the pickup at all until it was too late."

Her gaze lingered on the copse of trees and the small farmhouse he'd been ogling earlier. "What were you doing out here, Jesse?"

There it was. The reason he shouldn't have veered off his path one single foot. "I missed a turn and decided to roam for a bit. It's not like I have anything else going on today."

"No job?" Murphy's growl cut into their conversation.

Jesse would've shot him a glare, but his eyes might cross trying. He stuck with scowling at the ground. Gravel crunched over his shoulder and either his vision was going, imagining a second set of blue-and-red lights dancing across the ground, or it was another vehicle with a light bar.

He craned his head over his shoulder, ignoring the tinges in his neck. A slight woman with ink-black hair rushed toward him with a rectangular duffel bag in her hand.

"Deputy James. What have we got?" The woman's accent wasn't thick. She must be from somewhere in Asia. Did she feel like as much of an outsider as he did?

She squatted next to him and he read her nametag. She was a Walker.

For fuck's sake. He couldn't get away from them. Cursing his curiosity, he let her go through her routine, checking his pupils, asking about the accident and what he remembered. The Walker paramedic was brusque, efficient, and didn't seem to know who he was with respect to the Walkers. Farah rose to speak with the second member of the ambulance crew.

More lights splashed across the scene. More rushing footsteps.

His quick, unobtrusive trip in and out of Moore hit total-failure levels.

Jesse made out Caleb's familiar face as he approached the scene with the rest of his crew. They were in full fireman regalia, down to the boots.

Caleb's eyes widened when his gaze landed on the crowd around Jesse. He tensed. How would the man react?

It's not like they were friends or anything. After prison, Jesse didn't have friends. They had either ditched him if they were decent people, or he'd distanced himself from them to keep from getting drawn into more illegal activity.

Jesse switched his attention to the Walker paramedic he'd heard Farah call Dalisay. She squatted down next to him. "Do you still feel dizzy?"

He nodded. Might as well not lie. They'd all find out soon enough if he tried to stand and busted out an accidental cartwheel or some shit.

"I think you should go to the hospital and get checked out for a concussion." He appreciated that she sounded concerned instead of suspicious. But the hospital?

With what money? "Um, no. Thanks for everything, but I'm good."

The paramedics exchanged looks with Farah. Between the three of them, Farah was the only one who didn't look surprised.

The male paramedic tried again. "I really think you should let us transport you to the hospital."

Jesse chuckled. "The same thing said by a guy isn't going to make me change my mind."

A strangled snort came from Farah, but when they all glanced at her, she had already spun toward Caleb.

The paramedic slapped his thighs as he stood. "All right then. We have a release for you to sign and we're outta here."

What weird twist of fate made it more desirable to spend time around Walkers than other people in town? His sister.

The Walker paramedic. Soon, instead of avoiding them, he'd be hoping they invited him to dinner.

The older man trekked through the field toward his tractor like the uneven soil was as smooth as a walking path.

Farah and Caleb had been joined by the other firefighters and were deep in discussion. Jesse was alone.

He heaved out a breath and stared at his pickup. Four wheels pointed toward the sky, the box partially propped by the ditch edge to make it an even line. That was his sole streak of luck for the morning. He could've landed off-kilter, or dented the roof and door, making escape nearly impossible, or he could've smashed his head in.

Farah strode back to him as the firefighters went back to their rig. "Have you called Josie already?"

"God, no. She doesn't need to deal with this."

A blond brow lifted. Farah turned back to study the over-turned vehicle. "What's your plan, then?"

"Fuck." He rubbed his eyes, easing up on the pressure to keep from worsening the throb. "I guess I'll have to call her and see if she and Brock have the equipment to tow this."

Someone approached from his right. He jerked his head around. Caleb?

"Hey, man. Whatcha gonna do?"

"Yeah" was all Jesse could say. God, he hated adding more stress to Josie's life after he'd vowed to do better by her.

Caleb squatted down. "I got a proposition."

Jesse stilled because deals weren't usually in his favor. Farah's eyes narrowed and she hooked her fingers over her tactical belt.

Caleb continued, speaking like the three of them were in on a conspiracy. "I don't like that black truck story of yours."

Jesse bristled. He knew it. They didn't believe him.

Before he could get indignant, though, Caleb continued. "While you and Josie work on getting your wheels back on the ground, why don't you stay at my place? Recuperate. Fix your ride, but the main thing, call me if you ever see this truck again. In fact, list every vehicle and when you see them."

Jesse's incredulity grew with each word. Anger that no one trusted him died to disbelief that Caleb would help him again—and self-recrimination because dammit, Jesse really needed a hand.

"Caleb," Farah breathed and took a knee to add to their huddle.

The fireman held up a hand. "I get it, Farah. But your cows didn't get out last week because a twenty-foot stretch of brand-new fence suddenly failed. And I know three of my heifers weren't beamed up by aliens." His expression filled with intent. "We both know without saying who's behind this."

"So you're going to recruit Jesse to spy? Do you know what he's—" She slapped her lips together.

Jesse rolled his eyes. "What she's trying to say is how do you know I won't burn your place down and invite the whole town to a free steak barbecue?"

"Are you planning on it?" Caleb asked.

Jesse scoffed and looked away. His didn't want to see the distrust lingering in Farah's eyes.

"It won't matter who's fucking with us," Farah hissed. "If he's here, they'll find a way to frame him. This is a bad idea."

Was she…worried about him? "You know who ran me off the road?"

Caleb nodded once at the same time Farah said, "No."

"Someone's lying here and it's not me."

A guy hollered for Caleb from the fire engine.

Farah sighed. "We have no proof, only suspicions."

"I'll explain it all in the morning when I get home," Caleb said. "Farah can give you a ride and let you into my place.

Get some rest, don't destroy shit. We'll discuss our terms in the morning." He jogged off before Farah could argue.

This was crazy. Farah was right. Jesse could get dragged into their drama and be stuck looking like the guilty one. But his only other choice was to call Josie, and he refused to complicate her idyllic life. She'd dealt with enough of his problems.

He turned toward Farah, the move amplifying the throbbing in his head. The promise of some rest and a quiet place to think through his situation made the decision for him.

CHAPTER 4

Farah ignored the man next to her as she drove the mile to Caleb's place. They had keys to each other's homes and often kicked back a couple of cold ones as they lamented over their lands' sad state of affairs. Caleb was trying to limp along on his grandparents' ranch after they'd died and his mom and dad had ditched Moore and Minnesota altogether. Farah was trying to keep both feet out of bankruptcy. After her mom's stroke, her dad had let the hired help go to afford care for her. A couple of hard years and low cattle prices, and now they were struggling right next to Caleb.

She turned into the narrow dirt road that wound through to Caleb's house.

"You two are close, huh?" Jesse asked.

"We're friends." Things would've been easier if they liked each other as more than friends. But he was hung up on the one that got away and she was married to her job. "You gonna tell me what you were really doing by my place?"

She tightened her grip on the wheel, mentally preparing

for his indignation or hostility. Yet again, he surprised her by closing his eyes and resting his aching skull on the headrest.

"I told you what I was really doing." He opened one eye to peek at her. "I'm surprised you didn't make me ride in the back."

"Don't make me regret my decision."

One corner of his lips curled up. Prying her gaze off him was way harder than it should've been. In jail, he'd had the dangerous-bad-boy feel so many women found appealing. She'd been the only female he'd had access to, and she'd been ridiculous to let his intensity worm its way under her skin. Yet outside of jail, it was doubly hard to protect her lonely heart when he looked and talked to her like she was the only girl on the planet.

He seemed like just a guy who'd had a shitty day and was fighting a headache. He'd lost his hat in the accident and his ink-black hair was inviting enough to run her hands through. Her palms tingled with the idea.

"You're going to be stiff in the morning," she blurted, looping around Caleb's driveway. She parked by the back of his house with her car facing out.

"What?" He lifted his head and there was the scrutiny again, all on her. She opened the door to keep the enclosed cab from feeling too intimate, a problem she'd never had in her work vehicle.

"The whiplash. It'll be like you went a few rounds inside a washing machine."

He straightened from the vehicle, reminding her how tall he was. And how much she liked it. Jesse didn't use his size to swagger and intimidate like Clinton.

She popped the trunk and together they wrestled his rectangular blue metal toolbox to the ground, where she left it. He didn't insist it be moved anywhere else.

"Speaking from experience about the whiplash?" He

followed her up the few steps to Caleb's house, carrying a ratty black backpack over his shoulder. The three worn wooden steps creaked under his weight more than hers.

"Other people's, not me personally." She dug her personal key ring out of her pocket and opened the screen door. The hinges' creaking echoed through the yard.

"I can handle feeling rough. A broken neck would've been harder to come back from."

She paused pushing the door open, the remnants of her fear flaring up. When she'd driven up to the scene and seen his truck upside down... The dispatcher had relayed Murphy's information, but she'd rolled up to too many accidents that were more severe than the caller had thought.

Then there'd been the utter relief and the "thank God" leaving her lips when Murphy had shifted enough to reveal Jesse planted on the edge of the road.

She shook off her emotions. "Go call Josie. I'm sure the news has made it to the Walkers by now. Then crash on the couch." She stepped aside to make way for Jesse to enter.

He adjusted his backpack and entered, looking around at the small entryway with a narrow coat rack and an old powder room. Straight ahead was the door to the stairs to the basement. The couch was through a kitchen that was stuck in the seventies with paneled maple cupboards and faded yellow linoleum. The rusted white fridge was the most updated part of the room.

"Don't eat whatever's growing in the fridge." She should just leave, but there was one thing she had to talk to him about. And it wasn't freaking food poisoning, but it was a safe place to start and required less explanation.

Jesse was frowning at the fridge.

Farah stepped back inside. On a working ranch, no matter how poorly it worked, the warming weather meant flies were increasing in number. "It's so old, Caleb barely trusts it to keep his beer cold. He usually grabs something in town."

His eyes darkened. "Just friends that know each other's eating habits?"

She shoved down the swirl of delight at his male interest and scowled. "He's like a brother. Our parents would've loved for us to get married but if we haven't even kissed by now, then it's not going to happen." Why'd she even bother defending herself? Because she and Caleb had been doing so for so many years. It was none of Jesse's or anyone else's business.

He hadn't moved, but to get inside far enough to shut the door, she ended up far too close to him.

Looking up, she jumped on the real subject she'd meant to talk to him about. "When you call Josie, can you just leave it at lending Caleb a hand and not bring up our problems?"

One blink. Two blinks. His expression remained blank. "That might require a little more explanation before I lie to my sister."

"I didn't ask you to lie. We don't know for sure someone destroyed my fence or stole Caleb's cattle." The look he gave her was full of *do you think I'm stupid?* He was the felon Caleb had asked to watch over things, after all. "Look, our land borders…another family's with a large ranch. It's no secret we're struggling but determined to hold on to what belongs to us."

He crossed his arms, bringing her attention to the width of his chest. The orange jumpsuit hadn't done him justice, but this T-shirt was excellent. "And if you two fail and have to sell, this unnamed family"—he gave her a pointed look—"can snatch it up for rock-bottom prices and expand."

Exactly. And she hadn't said Clinton was the greedy bastard. Jesse might revert to his old ways, thinking to right a wrong. She didn't want him in trouble again, and certainly not because of Clinton. Her ex had to be the reason she'd become so protective of Jesse. She wouldn't hate herself if Jesse got himself into trouble. But she couldn't have Jesse face the consequences of her personal conflicts.

She lifted a shoulder. "It's obvious when shit happens while I'm working. My dad can't be everywhere." He was in town for Mom's therapy a lot and that was also predictable. The clinic wanted regular appointments not made at random times and what could Dad say? *But I'm afraid I'm being watched and I'll come home to missing cows.* "Caleb's shifts don't change. You hanging around just might be enough to scare the vandals off."

His eye twitched at the word vandal. Because he was one. But the more she was around him, the easier it was to forget his unlawful past.

"I'm not gonna be sitting around. I'll fucking vacuum or whatever until Caleb comes back and puts me to work. I'm going to earn my keep while my pickup gets fixed."

"I doubt Caleb can afford to pay you."

He grimaced, then shrugged it off. "I owe him anyway for letting me crash here."

"If you're handy around the house like you are with cars, then you'll find plenty to do. Or hell, see if you can get his haying tractor working. That'd pay him back for a month of staying here."

Jesse's eyes lit up. "Is it the one by the barn?"

She thought he'd had his eyes closed driving up, but he'd taken it all in. "Yes, the orange Kubota. I doubt it's seen an oil change for a decade."

He smiled, his gaze warming and relaxing for the first time since the accident.

Her belly clenched and she grasped for the door handle behind her. "Call if you need anything." She rushed outside.

No luck. Jesse caught the door before it slammed shut. "I don't have your number. Or Caleb's."

She didn't stop until she got to her car door. Pulling out her phone, she pulled up the contacts. "Gimme yours and I'll text you ours."

He rattled off his number. She keyed it in, sent him a quick wave, and managed not to spray gravel in her rush to put distance between her and Jesse.

All her life, she'd prided herself on being the one to run into dangerous situations, but that sexy man was a whole different level of trouble. Time to retreat.

JESSE STOOD BACK from the all-terrain vehicle Caleb called a side-by-side because it had two seats and a small box to haul tools and supplies. The little two-seater looked like a golf cart on steroids. Caleb cranked the key. When the motor purred to life, he let out a whoop.

"First try!" Caleb grinned. "You're totally worth your weight in the pennies I'm paying you. What'd you do?"

What Caleb offered to pay was enough to get by and settle the one debt Jesse had hanging over his head. But the work was as welcome as the income.

He tipped his cap back to let the breeze cool off his forehead. It wasn't even June yet and the temp was approaching eighty. "If I tell you my secret, then I'm out of a job."

"Ha! You'll never be out of work around here."

Wasn't that the truth. It'd been a week since the accident. Between Josie and Caleb, he'd been coerced into scrapping his totaled truck and saving the insurance payout and the meager funds Caleb offered to pay him for real labor. Once he built up a good amount, he could buy a cheap truck and take his time finding a job that wouldn't land him back in jail by association.

He should've argued more, used the excuse of his pride and ditched town. But he'd burned his pride with Dillon's shop and any shreds remaining were toasted when Josie had asked him to imagine her in the place of Dillon's grandma.

What if Brock passed away? Would Jesse expect Josie to turn everything over to the Walkers? She had nowhere else to go, no decent family nearby. What would she do? If she were fortunate enough to find love again and remarry—after tending to the property and fighting to make it profitable— should she give it all up?

Josie had made her damn point. And since she was all he had left, and Caleb and his ranch were only ten miles across the highway from her, he didn't fight it.

His ready acceptance had nothing to do with Caleb's elusive neighbor either.

He'd only heard from Farah once, the evening she'd dropped him off. She'd called and said, "Okay, you didn't die," because she'd been worried when Caleb hadn't checked in.

The stiffness she'd warned him about had been no joke. He'd suckled an ibuprofen bottle for two days as he hobbled around Caleb's, mentally prioritizing what he could see needed to be done.

The place was old and rundown.

But all of that got shoved to the side when it came to the cows. He'd come to think of them as walking dollar signs. It was his new duty to keep an eye on them when Caleb pulled his twenty-four.

Every few hours, Jesse drove the pastures with the old beat-up truck he'd rescued for Caleb to make sure no cattle were missing or wandering outside of the fence, which he also inspected. Now that they had the side-by-side fixed, he could cruise the pastures faster. Which was exactly what they were heading off to do.

Cows stopped grazing to stare as they drove by the weathered prairie trail. Waking up to cattle lowing was harder to get used to. Prison was loud. Every sound echoed off the hard floors, and cell doors clanged. His hometown was a normal town. There was always an engine running somewhere. Out here, the noisemakers were cows and birds. Sometimes horses, but Caleb didn't have any. Farah had two and when one started in, the other wouldn't let up, until Jesse wondering if an equine bouncer was needed.

Caleb popped into the driver's seat. Jesse got in next to him. They would stop periodically and hop out to inspect the fence, only Caleb looked much closer than Jesse did. The fastenings were inspected along the length of each post, and they walked short sections, studying the entire distance.

One sagging section left Caleb scowling and rubbing his chin. With the guy's worn jeans, work boots, and ball cap, he looked more like a farm kid and not the alt rock image he usually gave off.

Jesse was even blending in well. Josie had brought him a couple pairs of jeans. "These won't be destroyed within a week like your normal ones." She claimed his typical work boots were okay, but he often wore his athletic shoes. T-shirts should be okay, too, but no. Josie unloaded a whole bin of tops of varying thickness. Most were long-sleeved and button-up.

"Won't these be hot?" he'd asked.

"They don't call them farmer tans for no reason. Save your skin."

From what?

He'd found out the first time he'd snagged a sleeve on a piece of wire. The fabric tore, not his skin.

Jesse switched his attention back to the fence. It wasn't sagging as much as bowed in. "What caused that?"

"Usually, I'd say it's from the girls scratching themselves. And it could be." Caleb's gaze lifted to where Farah's land was. Her pastures bordered Caleb's until they both butted up against Clinton's land. "But when Farah's cows got out, it almost looked like someone had rammed the fence until a whole section collapsed."

Jesse ground his teeth together. That was a dick move. This was someone's livelihood. The irony he'd think that way now… He'd once interfered with someone's ability to earn a living. Jesse had been on the way to destroying Dillon Walker's expensive truck when he was busted. Now here he was, rage boiling through his veins that the same thing was happening to Farah. But he'd been aware of the damage and stress he'd caused through his sister. Seeing it firsthand happen to someone he cared about—well, Farah had always been fair and hardworking. He didn't have to like her to know that.

Too bad he could no longer deny liking her.

"I don't get it." Jesse rerouted his thoughts to the whole turf war going on. "Farah's a cop. You're a fireman. You both think something illegal is going on. Why aren't the sheriff and deputies out here investigating?"

Caleb's jaw tightened.

Jesse shook his head. Secrecy. His ass was on the line as much as theirs, probably more with his record. Had he been hired to take the fall? To be the target?

Jesse stomped back to the side-by-side when Caleb said, "Farah said Clinton was in the area that day."

Jesse stopped and turned. He didn't want to act too eager for answers, but he also didn't know how to wrestle fifty head of cattle back into a fence. Prevention would be best, but he needed a clue about what he was up against.

"Doesn't Clinton live out here?" Jesse assumed the other drivers he'd passed weren't felons taking the back roads home.

"Not as far out as where you saw him. His dad is my boss."

Oh. "Can't exactly go to the cops saying the fire chief's son is a criminal?"

"We all know it. Or have heard stories, thanks to Farah."

"The pepper spray?"

Caleb grinned and he practically danced around like a five-year-old who'd pulled the perfect prank. "It was epic. Clinton thought he was going to get some and she *hosed* him."

"What happened?" And had pepper spray been enough?

"She didn't tell you the whole story? I guess the whole town knows so it's okay if I tell you. Because it never gets old. Farah caught wind the idiot was going to live stream their prom night for his friends. She hit record on her own phone and when she busted him with his phone on record, she let 'er rip. The way he squealed, you woulda thought there was a pig in the room instead of an eighteen-year-old boy. She uploaded the footage just like he'd planned to."

"Did she get in trouble?"

Caleb's expression grew serious. "Almost got suspended. But her mom was the sheriff and Farah was only sixteen. Between her age and the intent to record, shit didn't look good for Clinton, and his dad is smarter than he is."

"He's still got a thing for Farah."

"I think his ego demands retribution, whether it's to finally have a go at her, or break her heart, or control her, who knows. But she's on his radar and since her mom's stroke, he's been doing some sort of weird mating dance around Farah. Like he's caught between trying to marry her for her property or running her out of business because he wants it all."

"Or he's using his affection as a smoke screen. If you both are getting messed with, then it looks less pointed than him trying to court her and destroy you."

Caleb ducked his head. "My boss is one thing, but Farah is… You know, she's the town's pride, but her coworkers tend to coddle her, not treat her as an equal. If she can't handle her own personal drama, it'll look bad for her. We need proof—what and who. Otherwise, imagine if we go to the sheriff and we're wrong? It'll backfire on her and me."

And without their jobs and the benefits that came with it, their ranches would fail. Jesse didn't have to grow up in this industry to know that. Caleb was barely surviving out here. Jesse had declared the fridge broke as hell yesterday and the oven couldn't be trusted to cook a frozen pizza. Jesse had found out the hard way after an hour and only soggy pepperoni to show for it. If the microwave hadn't been invented, they would have both starved.

Caleb's gaze lifted over Jesse's shoulder and his usual lighthearted self was back. "Speak of the damn devil." He cupped a hand around his mouth and yelled, "She's looking good."

Jesse spun around. Some of his old buddies still had the stereotypical swimsuit calendars hung up in their shops. Jesse had never had a place to call his own, so he'd never thought twice about what he'd hang. But suddenly, he was picturing the May model as a blond in a tank top on top of a reddish-brown horse. Her body swayed gently with each step. The ugly brown deputy cap was gone, replaced by a pink and black one that her ponytail stuck out from.

The seventies-style uniform pants were gone, too, replaced by soft jeans. He wanted nothing more than to see how well they molded over her curves as she dismounted.

He was accustomed to seeing her with items strapped around her torso, whether it was just the tactical belt when she was a jailer or as a deputy with the vest and belt. While he doubted she was completely unarmed—it didn't seem her style—she was as good as naked to him. Her light-pink tank top only showed off the swell of her breasts and her tanned skin.

Where were her long-sleeved shirts?

He almost stripped his off to cover her and not because he was a prude, but because he had no wish to see that golden skin marred.

Her gaze drifted over him, the corners of her mouth turned down. Never one to care about his appearance—people judged him based on his looks if not his clothing choices, so why bother? But he almost shuffled his feet to relieve the case of nerves he was stricken with. Was she going to laugh at his attempt at farm-boy chic? Had Josie been messing with him and this wasn't really what ranchers wore?

Well, he wasn't a rancher. He would always be a mechanic first. He was just a sub for Caleb.

Farah's gaze switched to Caleb. The horse snuffled as they approached.

How could a horse be this quiet up close and so stinking loud in the morning? "Is she one of the loud ones?"

Farah cocked her head, a line forming between her brows. Then she tossed her head back and laughed. "God, yes. She's been recovering and hasn't been a happy camper. She takes her aggression out on my mom's horse. She's ready to ride again, so I'm walking them both today so maybe I can sleep in tomorrow."

Farah stopped several feet away, but Caleb crossed to the horse and let her nuzzle and smell him before curling his arm under the mare's head to scratch her other cheek.

Jesse had to reconcile his jealousy at the companionship of the two friends. It was absurd to turn green over Caleb's familiarity with a horse. Jesse could pet the horse if he wanted.

He'd just never touched a horse. Did they get petted?

Josie had offered to take him riding, but he wasn't around enough and they rarely left the garage when he did visit. Because he'd had no interest in horses.

Suddenly he wanted to know everything about the beasts.

"Lily Fields," Caleb purred into the horse's ear, "you need to shut the hell up in the mornings."

She nickered in a way that sounded like *yeah, right.*

"What was wrong with her?" Jesse asked mostly to keep from standing awkwardly like a big sign reading *City Boy* hung over his head.

"Colic." A shadow flickered over Farah's face. "Her trough went dry for a couple days."

"Like it was tipped," Caleb muttered. "Even though Farah fills it each day."

Bastards. "How would hurting your horse benefit Clinton?"

Farah shot Caleb a pointed look, but Caleb shrugged. The guy spoke openly to him about what he thought Clinton and his brother were up to.

She needn't worry. Jesse wasn't one to spread rumors.

"Money. If Lily Fields had needed surgery, I might have had to…" Her eyes glistened and she looked away.

Caleb left the horse to cross the fence. "Farah doesn't have a working four-wheeler. She inspects her land on horseback."

"So taking a horse out does double duty."

Farah shrugged. "The horses could've tipped it."

"And set it back up?" Caleb interjected.

"Or the water could've evaporated."

"This time of year?" Caleb pointed to the fence. "It's hard to tell, isn't it? Just like it's hard to tell if three cows had sudden itches on their bellies at the same time and lined up to rub against the fence or if a pickup gave it a nudge along the post."

As Farah swung down from Lily Fields, Jesse almost gave himself another case of whiplash watching her sinuous strength. Muscles rippled through Farah's shoulders and back, her ass rounding in a spectacular way as she landed on the ground and lowered her leg from the stirrup.

She was a good eight inches shorter than him, but she wasn't tiny. She wasn't going to blow away, but she wasn't as bulky as her uniform made her seem. Her size was… It was like he could feel her pressed against him, his hands on her hips, his—

He cleared his throat and turned back to Caleb.

Tall grass whispered behind him as Farah led the horse to Caleb. The mass of the creature passed him and he couldn't stop his hand from lifting. This lifestyle was new, but it called to him. Was this how his dad had felt? Why he'd spent so many days fishing until it'd become his demise?

As Jesse's finger grazed over the silky, solid hide and the musky scent of horse wafted over him, he tried to brush away the thought of his dad, but he couldn't. Dad had loved fishing, especially from a boat, where he could get better catch, but he hadn't been comfortable enough with swimming to take Jesse. *When you're older* had turned into never because a life jacket hadn't been enough for Dad.

Lily Fields quit moving. Jesse glanced at Farah. She was watching him.

He snatched his hand back. "I don't… Horses…"

"Go ahead and pet her. She's only pissy with her sister at the moment." Farah loosened the lead rope and Lily Fields's mighty head swung around until she gazed at Jesse with a dark eye.

He scratched her rough cheek like Caleb had. She

swiveled her head away and he let his hand glide down her neck. The power underneath his fingers… A smile played at his lips and he let out a soft chuckle.

Farah glanced back at him.

"Horse power. Now I finally get it." All those years of commenting on the horses under a hood and here he was in awe of an actual horse. What about those big ones from the beer commercials?

Farah smiled. "My grandpa used to work this land with horses, even after tractors were common, because he already had the horses." She stepped around the front of Lily Fields to inspect the fence. "A blanket draped over the fence would protect a paint job, and just saying…" She pointed down the uneven, busted trail that he and Caleb had taken. "If you keep going, you'll come out right where Jesse was run off the road."

Jesse abandoned the horse and went to the fence line to gaze down. The first thing he'd done when he'd recovered was cover the length of the trail, but he hadn't put that together with the weak spot in the fence.

She put her hands on her hips. Jesse wanted that pose for June. "But cattle getting out happens to all ranchers. We need something more concrete."

Caleb caught Jesse's eyes. "Well, we know what we're fixing today."

Jesse didn't know the first thing about repairing a fence. Looked like he was going to learn.

"Why don't I bring out lunch when I take Petunia for a ride?"

Jesse's brows popped. Today was the first time they'd been around each other outside the realm of law enforcement. And she wanted to come back even though he was going to be here?

"Is it sandwiches on your mom's homemade bread?" Caleb asked.

The easy question clarified Farah's willingness to feed them. She and Caleb must do this all the time.

Only the corner of Farah's mouth lifted. Sadness simmered in her gaze. "Mom uses a bread machine now, but it's still better than store bought."

"Everything your mom makes is better than store bought."

Jesse's stomach growled. The idea of homemade food was going to drive him insane faster than his year of hard time. His own mom had been an excellent cook, and she'd made sure he and Josie were proficient in the kitchen. But Jesse had to have a kitchen—with working appliances—in order to use his skills.

Farah lifted her chin. "I'll finish my rounds and grab the food." She rounded Lily Fields to the same side she'd dismounted on. The horse lifted her head from her idle munching.

Farah swung up so quickly and easily he'd blinked and missed it. Damn. Shifting the reins, she guided Lily Fields to continue on her way. He forced himself not to stare after her.

"I shoulda packed the tools," Caleb said, "but we can inspect more area on our way back."

Why hadn't they packed the tools? Jesse wouldn't make that mistake again. He hated delaying projects because he was running around finding his equipment, but that seemed to be Caleb's MO. The guy was scatterbrained.

He hoped that didn't extend to payday. Jesse was prepared to remind him. A regular paycheck was a necessity. His one personal debt was a doozy.

He glanced back at Farah. She was coming back with homemade food, and he couldn't pinpoint which he was more excited about.

CHAPTER 5

Farah stuffed the last sandwich into the container. A shuffling patter scraped across the hardwood behind her.

"A picnic shhounds divine." Mom's slow speech and slurred *s*'s fractured her heart.

Farah smiled as her mom braced an arm on the counter next to her. To anyone else it might look like a casual stance, but for her mom, it was a test of balance. She'd graduated from a walker to a four-legged cane, but the fall factor was a constant fear.

"Want to eat before I go?" The ham and cheese would be too much for Mom to chew without being cut up first, but Farah could slather jelly on the bread that had survived her sandwich-making frenzy.

The left side of mom's mouth tipped up. Her new smile since the stroke. Not as much function had returned on her right side as they'd hoped—yet.

"Your father's eating with me." She stopped to swallow. A sentence that should take two seconds to say was stretched out past five. A solid part of her therapy was speech therapy, including learning to swallow properly again. Mom tipped her head to the lunch bags. "Caleb?"

"Yeah." Farah paused, loading the chips into the food bag. "He and Jesse are working on a section of fence. They've been monitoring our land, too, so I thought I'd bring 'em lunch. You know how Caleb is."

"Forget his head if it wasn't attached." She straightened off the counter, carefully placing her cane under her. Her right arm curled back to her side. Once her dominant arm, her firing arm, it was now a daily fight to keep the muscles from atrophying. "Anything new?"

Farah had to clear her throat of the emotion clogging it. Mom was probably dying to have a long conversation and ask a million questions. But talking took such effort, she'd taken to shortening everything she said.

"Not that we know of. I'm taking Petunia this afternoon and we'll look at the rest, but the bull pasture was fine." Bulls getting loose were more of a concern for her than the cows. "Calves are getting big."

"How… Caleb'shh help?"

How was Jesse? The question Farah had asked herself too much.

"He's been doing good. No signs of malice. He's already gotten Caleb's side-by-side running and done the morning chores a few times."

Mom stared at her. It'd been no use to keep the details about Jesse secret. Mom and Dad were in town too much and gossip about Jesse spread as fast as the fire that he'd lit in Dillon's shop.

"I'm not vouching for him, Mom, but right now Clinton seems like the bigger danger."

Mom's keen gaze was full of calculation. She'd been congenial with their neighbors, but Clinton's dad had subtly undermined Mom's work, whether it was going through the male deputies for inquiries instead of her or being vocal about his thoughts on nepotism and Farah's job with the county. Once Fire Chief Bradford learned that the county had not only reelected Mom as sheriff, but also that most thought Farah being a deputy was more than cute, he'd started insinuating her not-a-man size affected her ability to protect the county's fine citizens.

His behavior was nothing less than Farah had expected, but she'd still lost sleep over it.

So had Mom. She finally nodded. "You're good at character. But watch him."

Oh, she was watching Jesse all right. Not being able to take her eyes off him was half her problem. She also saw enough to know that he was trying to pretend that the anger that had gotten him into trouble didn't exist, and in her line of work, she was well aware of what happened when avoidance failed. Jesse might want to walk on the right side of the law for his sister, but he had to want to change himself for himself. Until then, he couldn't really deal with the festering issues that ate away at his conscience in the first place. If they did. She shouldn't be romanticizing his emotions.

She closed up the lunch bags and hefted them off the counter. Her only concern was feeding Jesse and Caleb, not psychoanalyzing them. She was a cop, not a shrink.

Dad strode into the square kitchen in all his bowlegged glory. "It's going to be a hot one today. I closed all the windows before the temp inside matches the temp outside. There's no such thing as a cool wind this time of year."

Another attempt to get through the day without AC. Dad was frugal, but it was more of a necessity now than habit.

"Where you going, kid?" His voice grew deeper and rougher each year. If someone wanted a model for an old rancher, her dad would make an ideal subject. His light-brown hair was buzzed short, shocks of gray at each temple, and topping off the look was a pair of reading glasses hanging around his neck.

She grinned as she edged toward the back door with her haul. "Welfare check, Dad."

His laugh was like rocks over sandpaper. He'd always called checking on the calves doing welfare checks. The play on words had made Mom giggle.

Heading to the barn where she'd already corralled Petunia, she couldn't take her mind off her parents and how she wanted what they had. They each had tough jobs. Mom had come home morally destroyed over what she'd witnessed on duty, but Dad had been her pillar. Same when a freak spring blizzard had decimated half their cattle numbers. Mom had rolled up her sleeves and pushed forward instead of wallowing in what the weather had stolen from them.

Farah's work didn't make it easy to meet prospective love interests. Dealing with the criminals and dark-hearted people in the area didn't leave her much time to get out and mingle with the decent ones. Then she couldn't help trying to determine if her dates were lying to her or had their own hidden agendas, the cop persona hard to put away after a long day. It didn't exactly leave her hyped for dating.

Then there was Jesse. She would've said at one time he was dark hearted. The fury that fueled him had been undeniable. But even before he'd left the county jail for prison, he'd simmered down. Being locked up while his sister was at the mercy of her dad's stupid plans must have altered his thinking.

She gave Petunia a low whistle. The mare barely twitched, displeased that she'd been taken out of the pasture. Farah had even saddled her already, unwilling to do it when she had an armload of food. Petunia only played at well-behaved when she was saddled. The harrowing minutes before often made Farah reconsider how important it was to keep her ridden.

But giving up on riding Mom's horse was like admitting that Mom would never be well enough to ride again. Technically, Mom could ride anytime. The snow was gone and she was down to a cane, but when Farah had brought it up, the sharp shake of Dad's head had stolen her suggestion.

She tucked the food into the saddlebags and strapped the lunchbox to the back of the saddle. That earned a nicker from the horse.

Farah swung up and maneuvered the cranky beast out of the barn.

The breeze with its hint of spring coolness was the only thing saving the day from being uncomfortably warm. She tugged her hat down and scanned her acreage as they rode. She absentmindedly counted cattle, a habit formed from the last few months of paranoia. The rest of her habits were from hanging on Dad's pant leg and being trained in all things cattle since she'd learned to walk.

Several minutes later, she rode up on the guys. Their shirts were plastered with sweat and the fence was nearly repaired. Jesse had rolled his sleeves up, and from this distance, the flex and twist of his forearms was clear—and heady. With the material of the shirt hugging his body, his shoulders appeared impossibly wider and his hips tapered into an admirable ass and powerful thighs. He was stockier than Caleb and only an inch taller, but Caleb had been wiry until he'd gotten his current job and started lifting regularly.

The two worked in harmony. Jesse didn't seem to have issues taking orders and following Caleb's lead. Both men had darker skin where hers was merely tanned, but Jesse's eyes were a lighter brown. Farah could describe them in detail. How they darkened when he was deep in thought or irritated. How they twinkled when he was teasing her, even when the rest of his body language made her think he was serious. How the lines of amber that striated each iris dazzled like chocolate diamonds when the sun caught his eyes under the brim of his hat.

The only way she'd describe Caleb's eyes were brown.

Why, Farah? Jeez. Of all the men she'd gone to school with and who'd passed through town, why be infatuated with Jesse?

When they spotted her, they straightened. Both put a hand on their stomachs, the looks on their faces telling her they were more excited about what she'd brought than her company.

She grinned. "Work up an appetite yet?" Wrapping her reins around the saddle horn, she snatched the lead rope and slid down Petunia. The horse was more than happy to graze in a new spot. Farah tied her off on a fence post.

Caleb was already raiding her saddlebags. "Yasss. Extra cheese, right?"

"If I've learned one thing growing up with you, it's your love of all things cheese."

They settled near the fence line. Petunia crunched on grass and the cattle stayed on the opposite end of the field. She lobbed calving numbers back and forth with Caleb.

"I'm gonna take a load in tomorrow," Caleb said. "Jesse can help me and see what selling's like."

Jesse's smile was sheepish. "I'm kinda looking forward to it. It's a whole new world."

Caleb started in on an explanation of loading cattle and what to expect at the stockyards. The whole time they'd been sitting and eating, something had dawned on her, and it wasn't how easily Jesse fit into their group. He listened, asked questions, joked around. His legs were kicked out in front of him, and the way he'd demolished her sandwich and chips made her feel like a five-star chef.

She switched to examining the fence.

She was scanning the length when Caleb broke into her thoughts. "You're wearing your cop face."

Jesse paused with the water bottle up to his lips, his eyes darting around. He must live with the constant paranoia of getting arrested again.

She nodded. "I can't help but think that we haven't had to worry about sitting in a pile of cow patties. If the cows were hanging here long enough to nearly push down the wire, then why isn't there more shit around?"

"Because it was fucking Clinton and his brother." At her admonishing look, Caleb waved it off. "Come on. It's just us out in the middle of nowhere. We know better than to say that in public, but out here, let's be honest. What else could he do to fuck with us?"

"I don't know what wouldn't be obvious." Actually, she could name twenty things Clinton could tamper with, ranging from cattle nabbing, to water tipping, to vandalism. But it'd make her crazy trying to plan for every scenario while worrying she'd still missed one. "We should get security systems for both our places. I've checked into them and there are some reasonably cheap options."

Caleb pointed at Jesse. "I hired security, remember?"

"He's a hired hand who can't be here twenty-four seven. What about when you're at the firehouse and it's three in the morning? What about when my parents are at therapy?"

Jesse gathered wrappers and baggies. "You guys buy it, I'll install it." He rose and her heart climbed in her throat. She was still on the ground and he towered over her, his face shadowed by the brim of his cap.

She liked it.

He backed away with his arms loaded. "I'm going to start heading back. We've been gone all morning and I told Josie I'd meet her this evening to look through auction sales for a cheap ride."

The walk would only take him twenty minutes, but he'd been working in the heat all morning.

She glanced at Caleb. He shrugged. "I told him I'd do another head count and he could take off. He's been glued here since he started." Caleb leaned over. "But really, Brock's grilling tonight and I think Jesse wants some real food."

"What broke now?" Farah asked.

"The oven turned Jesse's pizza into goo."

Farah giggled. Jesse was dangerously close to becoming a normal person. Not a felon, or a man she should stay away from, but a guy she was genuinely starting to like. His disapproval of Clinton seemed real and his handiwork could already be seen all over Caleb's place. The guys had driven the side-by-side, and Caleb's haying tractor was running now, too.

"I can give him a ride." She stood and brushed herself off.

"I doubt he's ever ridden a horse."

"And if he's gonna be here looking after our livestock, he should be comfortable around them." He'd touched Lily Fields like she was a magical creature from his dreams. Seeing horses off in the distance was one thing, but learning to ride one was another. Comfort and familiarity were critical for most ranchers.

Jesse had packed up all the remains of lunch. All she needed to do was swing onto Petunia and guide her toward Jesse.

He glanced over his shoulder, his gaze traveling the length of the horse. Did he realize how much his want was obvious? He was fascinated by horses.

"Hop on," she said as she rode even with him.

He looked at her like she'd suggested they race. "What?"

"Actually." She dismounted. "You should ride back."

He glanced from her, to the horse's back, laughed, and continued walking. She fell in step next to him, the lead rope loose in her hand. She knew Petunia well enough. The horse had never been a bolter. Yes, she could be ornery but she was well trained. Petunia was the horse Farah had learned to ride on.

"You're working on a ranch. You should know a little about horses."

He chuckled, the corners of his eyes crinkling. His laughter in jail had been full of derision and bitterness. She liked this kind of emotion in him better. It suited him.

"Caleb doesn't have horses."

"But I do and if his cattle get out—with help or not—his side-by-side isn't as agile as a horse. We use both to round up loose cattle and drive them back."

"He has a four-wheeler. It's my project for tomorrow."

It was on the tip of her tongue to ask if he'd work on hers, too, but he was Caleb's help. She tried another tactic, unable to explain why it was so important to get his ass on a horse.

Because her mom had always said part of what attracted her to Dad was how he handled his livestock—with respect, and when it came to horses, with total love and adoration.

"Haven't you ever wanted to ride?"

Another soft laugh escaped, but he kept walking. "I'm not getting my thirty-three-year-old ass up there and making a fool of myself."

She stopped. "Are you seriously worried about image in front of me?" She'd seen him in a cell and monitored him while he brushed his teeth.

He faced her, his expression contemplative. Yanking his hat up, he smoothed his hand over his glossy hair and considered Petunia. Farah's fingers itched to run through Jesse's hair. Every time, dammit.

"Petunia's the horse we use for beginners." Which would make her perfect for Mom to ride now, but that was a worry for another day. "I'll sit behind you."

His apprehension faded. Heat infused his eyes, darkening the irises. She hadn't fully thought out this plan when she'd first offered to teach him how to ride.

"You're going to sit up there with me?"

Farah fought not to swallow. "There's room behind the saddle. I'll hold the lunchbox."

"All right. What do I do?"

She guided him onto the saddle, showed him where to place his feet. Petunia shifted and Farah worried Jesse might launch off.

"Take a deep breath. You're not bothering Petunia."

"I know. It's just…" His hands gripped the reins.

Farah reached up, her breasts pushing into his leg as she readjusted his hand around the reins. She tapped his left hand. "Put that one on your thigh. This isn't an old western. You don't need both hands."

He did as he was told and blew out a breath. "Holy shit," he muttered.

She grinned. The reverence in his tone was so unlike the Jesse she'd first met. What had happened in his life that had led to him getting arrested?

"Hold still. I'm coming up." Petunia was an average-sized horse, but Farah had perfected climbing onto a horse without stirrups as soon as she was strong enough to get the vertical jump down.

She hauled herself up behind Jesse, the move not as smooth as she'd hoped because she didn't normally do this with someone in the saddle. She settled, getting used to the awkward sitting position with a lunchbox on her lap and bumpy saddlebags under her thighs. But it was worth it. Jesse's laundry-fresh scent and his natural heat surrounded her.

"Okay," she said, more breathless than she should be. "You

won't have to do much with Petunia. Just tap her flank with your heel."

He paused so long she wondered if he thought she was pulling his leg. Finally, he tapped her side.

Petunia meandered through the pasture. Farah explained how to use the reins and how to make Petunia go faster, which they wouldn't do or Farah might bounce off the ass end of her.

Jesse laughed, the sound almost boyish. "I don't see you bouncing, Deputy."

An unwelcome glow ignited in her belly. She was sitting too close to him, and the way he said Deputy... "Petunia would leave me in the weeds out of spite. She's well trained, but she's got an attitude."

"Sounds familiar."

"I like you better like this," she blurted. The glow puffed out.

His shoulders tensed. "I like me better like this, too," he said quietly.

"What happened?" For once, she was grateful for Petunia's slow pace.

"I thought you knew the reason."

"I heard about how Dillon's land used to belong to your family, but it stayed with his grandma when she was widowed. But I'm asking what happened to make you want that land back so badly."

"You know about Josie's problems with her dad?"

"He stole Brock's Mustang." She'd been working at the jail when Brock had come to see Jesse to find out what had happened to Josie. The fear in Jesse's eyes when he'd learned Brock couldn't get ahold of her stuck in Farah's memory. She'd thought it was the first time Jesse truly realized how he'd cut himself out of Josie's life and couldn't be around to help.

"Yeah, well, he was a piece of shit long before that. My dad…" They swayed together on Petunia's back. Farah didn't press him for more of an explanation. "My dad drowned when he was fishing one day. Ma didn't date forever and then suddenly she was married to Bill. He was a controlling bastard, and a cheater, but Ma stuck by him. Josie adored him until he treated her like her femininity made working on cars impossible."

"How was he with you?" Farah could guess. The domestic disturbances she was called to showed her all kinds of scenarios.

"An ass, but he wasn't bad. I didn't see it for the controlling tactics it was. I didn't go to school. 'You'll learn all you need on the job without the bills.' He picked what Josie got a degree in. 'I'm paying for it, my choice.'"

Jesse fell quiet again. The buildup to Jesse's breakdown was clear. What had the climax been? She wanted to rub his tight shoulders. The telling wasn't easy for him.

"I didn't notice all the digs either. He used to rub it in that my family had been swindled out of what was rightfully ours. That maybe my dad would still be alive if we'd been raised in Moore." He glanced over his shoulder again. Her heart tore at the ragged look in his eyes. "Ridiculous, I know. I wouldn't even be me if Grandma had stayed in Moore. But Bill used Dad's death against me." Jesse's head tipped down, like he was ashamed he'd fallen for a grown man's emotional manipulation when he'd only been a kid at the time.

"But I stayed and worked for Bill. I used to draw, you know. Entertained the idea of being a tattoo artist, but all that fell away. We grew his business together. I was good with the classics and people paid top dollar to have me work on their baby. I think he was jealous. Then Ma had a heart attack and died."

Farah inhaled. The terror she'd felt sitting by her own

mom's bedside, wondering if she'd pull through, was still fresh. "I'm sorry. What'd he do?"

Jesse snorted. "He cut me off. Said he was selling the garage to an obnoxious prick he'd set up with Josie. The guy was an ass to her, and Bill was going to reward him for it?" He shook his head. She could only peek at part of his profile, but he'd reverted back to the Jesse from jail. "Meanwhile, I had no savings. Bill had talked me into putting all my earnings back into the biz. I had no degree. What was I going to do? Walk door-to-door asking if they had a classic car that needed work? I had nothing. *Nothing.*" Jesse chuckled, regressing back to the humorless guy she'd first met. "Even my girlfriend at the time dumped me. And Bill made sure to repeatedly point out what little I had and what I could've had."

And Jesse had directed all that loss, anger, and pain toward Dillon.

"I hated him." Jesse glanced over his shoulder again. "Dillon, that is. Crazy, right? I hadn't even met him. And no matter what I did to him, he flourished. I ruined one tractor and he got a bigger, better one. I meant to start a little fire in his shop, and well, the whole town knows how that turned out."

"You didn't mean to destroy everything?" He had, though. So why did intention matter to her? She wasn't a lawyer.

"Shoulda known better, but it's not like I'm an expert in starting fires. I'd never even started a campfire before. I thought he'd see the flames and call the fire department. I didn't know his ass was passed out."

She'd been better off thinking he was a hardened criminal pretending to be a hardworking handyman. Her heart was melting. "What about Dillon's truck?"

Jesse barked out a laugh. Petunia's ears swiveled back.

"Want to know a secret?" He twisted around. "I didn't crash it into the campground."

"What?"

"Nope. I saw Elle haul his drunk ass into her car, so I moved his pickup and left it running to drain his gas. My guess is some delinquents broke into it. My shitty lawyer said no one was going to believe I was innocent of that."

His lawyer was right. "So you admit to hot-wiring it?" she teased.

"Hell, yes. I'd be a shitty mechanic if I couldn't start an engine without keys." His humor died.

"What about dumping gasoline on his truck?"

"It was an impulsive thing. I'd used up all my spray paint and didn't want to raise suspicion by buying more." He tilted his head and looked at the sky. "I was watching his girlfriend's place because I knew, just knew they were going to get back together, and sure enough, he shows up. Fuck, his life kept getting better and I was at such a low. I mean, I'm not a stalker, but there I was."

"Weren't you afraid the gas might ignite?"

He twisted around again. "Deputy, I'm disappointed. You don't usually tiptoe around topics."

Hurt resonated under the tease. "Fine. Were you going to start it on fire, too?"

He turned back to look ahead. "Maybe. I had no conscious inclination to, but it was in the driveway and not close to other buildings. I doubt it would've hurt more than his vehicle. It's not like I was using my brain. I was angry. He had my land, a new pickup, and the girl."

"You wanted Elle?" Elle was nice enough. Pretty, of course. And smart. Farah was not jealous.

"Meh. I tried hitting on her, thinking I could at least steal her away, but she didn't go for me. He got it all, no matter what I did. It was like history repeating itself. His family got everything that should've been my family's."

She tapped his shoulder. "Urge her toward Caleb's. She veering toward home."

He followed directions, gently shifting the reins until Petunia stayed on the path to Caleb's house.

"Perfect." She couldn't resist complimenting him. He didn't yank on the reins or overexaggerate the commands. Petunia was smart but entering her golden years and Farah was more than a little protective of her.

The white two-story house came into sight. They were parallel with the driveway. Petunia was comfortable enough on Caleb's property that Jesse didn't need to do anything more than tell her when to stop.

Farah wanted to squeeze more conversation in before they arrived at their destination. "And now? How do you feel about Dillon and Elle?" They had an adorable little boy and were expecting number two. The Walker Five were growing and doing well.

"You sound like my parole board. Like I told them, I'm worried about building my life back to the point where it's… mine again. I can't get my life back worrying about someone else."

She clamped her arms to her side; otherwise she might throw them around him and bury her face in his back. In her line of work, she heard a lot of excuses and it wasn't for her to determine whether they were valid or not. Jesse had broken the law. Several times. He could've seriously injured someone, and he'd been old enough to know better.

But he'd been hurting. He still was, only he was trying to be a better person. That she didn't often see. She had her repeat offenders. The ones who drove drunk time and again. The abusive spouses, parents who beat their kids. She wasn't around when they tried to improve themselves, if they even did. But she was there when they fucked up again.

They reached Caleb's yard. She wanted to keep talking, but if she didn't tell him what to do with Petunia, the horse would meander straight through the yard to find her own pasture.

"Tell her 'whoa' and tug back on the reins."

Petunia stopped. Farah hopped down. Jesse dismounted without any coaching, a subtle groan escaping him.

"A man's legs aren't supposed to be spread like that for so long."

Farah giggled. "Horses came before cars."

He handed over the reins, his fingers grazing her palm. "Ever wonder why dudes invented a car in the first place?"

"You're going to smell like horse sweat, too."

He smiled. The crinkles at the corners of his eyes went straight to her belly. "Just another reason to slide behind the wheel of a V8."

She chuckled. His sense of humor was a wicked surprise. Laughter hadn't come around often since Mom's stroke.

She couldn't take her eyes off his. They were standing close, Petunia creating a wall between them and the rest of the world.

Her lungs froze as his head dipped, angling to keep their caps from clashing. She couldn't move. Alarm bells should've gone off, but after his honest story, she saw the real him.

Common sense nearly rushed in and pushed her back, but his lips landed on hers first. She wasn't going anywhere.

For such a hard man, his lips were soft. The smell of his aftershave clung to his skin, a hidden surprise underneath the heady smells of sweat and horse.

He didn't advance, but lightly kissed her. The reins hung limp in one hand, but she clung to Jesse's shoulder with her other hand. His hard, muscular shoulder. What would he look like with his shirt off?

He wrapped his arms around her, his hands landing at her waist, fingers splaying to cover her lower back. She'd never felt as petite and feminine as she did now.

Hesitantly, his tongue swept across her lips and she was opening for him, a thrill coursing through her at getting to taste him. But Petunia nickered.

Reality crashed back.

She was a cop. He was a felon. She'd fought for her job, fought to be seen as a real police officer and not a figurehead the department used to claim it had fair hiring standards while swooping in to protect her whenever things got dangerous.

Jerking back, the brim of her cap hit his and knocked hers up. It didn't fly off thanks to the ponytail through the back, but she was grateful for the distraction while she straightened it.

"I, um, I can't…"

A shade crashed down over his expression. "I get it." He used his thumb to skim over her jaw. "Doesn't mean I haven't been dreaming about doing that since I saw you on the other side of my cell."

Her heart stuttered, torn between wanting to know what else he'd been dreaming about and triumph that she'd had that effect on a rugged guy like Jesse.

For God's sake, they'd met when he was in jail! She couldn't do this.

"My job." It seemed to be all she could say. She needed her work. It was the only thing keeping her family's ranch afloat.

He nodded, his eyes full of understanding. "I know." His tone added *I don't deserve you.* He stepped back, patting Petunia on the back before clearing her backside to walk toward the house. "When Josie drags me onto one of her horses, I'll pretend it's my first time."

She was going to tell him he didn't have to, but keeping the ride between the two of them and Caleb and Petunia protected him as much as her. Farah didn't know Josie well, but she was a sister and likely overflowing with concern and curiosity about her brother.

Lord knew, Farah had those feelings for Jesse, among so many others. His touch still burned on her lips. She wanted more. Her heart rate kicked up.

Never again. Mere chit-chat with him threatened her job, her credibility at the very least. He was a felon. But that chaste kiss? It could cost her her badge.

CHAPTER 6

"*O*h, you cranky bastard," Jesse muttered as he gave one more twist on the wrench. The oil plug refused to budge. He'd asked Caleb when the last time the oil had been changed in the John Deere riding lawn mower and the guy had shrugged.

Caleb's grandparents had died a few years ago, but the ranch and all the equipment with it had been neglected long before that. Between refusing to leave their home and not being able to afford senior care anyway, Caleb's grandparents had weathered their golden years out here, dying within weeks of each other.

Jesse should be grateful for the state of neglect around the place. Job security. The work was never ending. Yesterday was payday. His current income couldn't compare to working in an auto shop, even with the free room and board, and he had no benefits, but it was enough to write the checks he needed to send each month. Besides, he couldn't explain to himself why he wasn't willing to move on to find a better job, beyond that he liked it here.

And that his sister was here and she was due to have a baby in October. And he had nowhere else to go.

Waking up to the obnoxious robins squawking outside his window was a weird sort of peace. And he set his own pace and his own schedule. No pressure from management to game the system or squeeze just one more job into a day. Of course, Jesse had gotten paid the same hourly rate no matter how many alternators he'd installed.

But in all those years, he'd never met an oil plug as stubborn as this. He dropped the wrench with a clang. Looked like he was push mowing again.

Jumping up, he kicked the wrench across the floor for good measure.

"Fuck!" A tiny hunk of metal was derailing his plans.

Sucking in a breath, he closed his eyes. Ten, nine, eight… Undue anger toward the stuck plug faded with each beat.

I'm calm, I'm collected, I'm in control. At first, he'd felt silly repeating a mantra, but his unlikely mentor had threatened to paddle his ass if he didn't. And it hadn't been false bravado.

There. All better. He trudged over to where the tool had skittered and picked it up. While he was at it, he tidied all his tools. *Clean equals calm.*

He brushed himself off and checked his appearance. He needed to run to town to get parts in anticipation of destroying that plug. And he had a check to mail. And groceries. God, they needed groceries.

And a grill. Jesse was going to burn all his earnings, but it would be worth it to eat real meat again. Caleb had a chest freezer that amazingly was still working and full of quality cuts of meat. This was a ranch, after all. But they could do little more than nuke it in the microwave and that was just sad, even to a city boy like him.

Caleb claimed he was buying an oven when his shift was

over tomorrow, but still. It was steak. Wasn't it illegal to cook a T-bone in an oven?

He left his work where it was and ducked out of the standalone garage that had become his makeshift shop. Climbing into Caleb's old pickup, he rolled down the window. There was no AC and it was already seventy with no clouds by ten a.m. He was greasy; might as well be dusty, too.

Flying to town, he ignored the knot forming in his stomach. He avoided city limits as much as he could. Between the threat of passing the many Walkers in this area and the town's residents knowing who he was, it wasn't worth it. Caleb didn't need the trouble and Jesse didn't need a story to tell Josie when she asked if anyone was giving him any trouble. And she always asked.

He swung by the post office first, wasting a stamp on a check that would only travel a few miles. But it wasn't like he could hand deliver it. Next was the ATM for cash because he didn't want to flash his name all over with a debit card. Then the auto-parts store. He hadn't been back since he'd gotten the battery.

The AC hit him in the face as soon as he cleared the door. The smells of oil, grease, and plastic swamped him. His comfort zone. A few people milled around the store. One navy-blue cap in particular caught his eye.

A beat of relief hit him, and he tracked down Brock. "Hey, Brock. Josie in town?"

Brock's brows rose, but his expression remained amicable. Jesse liked that Brock let Josie set the tone for handling her felonious brother instead of letting the rest of the Walkers justifiably sway his opinion.

But then if Jesse hadn't gushed to Josie about the car collection he'd seen at Brock's place, Josie wouldn't have snuck onto Brock's property to see for herself and the two would've only seen each other in passing at Jesse's trial.

"She wanted to get some mowing done before the weather got too hot."

"That's what I had planned, but I'm still working on changing the riding lawn mower's oil."

Brock nodded and snagged a new windshield wiper blade from the thirty different brands and sizes to choose from. "Caleb's Chevy hasn't died on you yet?"

"Nah. A new battery and some TLC inside the engine and it's running fine. I was thinking of stopping by later."

Brock's blue eyes pinned him. "Better not. We're going to Travis's for a family barbecue tonight."

Gotcha. Brock was blunt, and his straightforwardness was refreshing. The guys Jesse usually came across—including his time in prison—were always trying to prove something at the expense of those around them. But Brock was in his own world, and Josie was safely ensconced within it. Jesse couldn't ask for more.

He would have to remind himself of that when he was eating his own grilled steak alone tonight.

"I'll call her, then. Tell her I said to put her feet up." Jesse grinned, not sure Brock would get the tease. Josie hated being told to take it easy. The baby was the perfect excuse to irritate her like a brother should.

Brock winced. "Will do, but I tried to tell her that this morning."

Jesse chuckled and turned around to locate the oil section and pick his plug. A man blocked his way, topping him by two inches. Clinton. The guy was as big as his obnoxious pickup.

Unconsciously, Jesse squared his shoulders and straightened. "'Scuse me." He tried to step around, but Clinton edged into his path.

"Didn't I see you the other day?"

It'd been two weeks since Farah had pulled over to check on his suspicious activity. Jesse didn't need the reminder about Farah. He'd been trying to forget her since that smoldering kiss. She was packing as much heat in her lips as she did when she was on duty.

A manipulative glint entered Clinton's eye. "Yeah. Farah had you pulled over."

Clinton's deep voice boomed through the store. He was as loud as his truck, too. Heads turned their way. Jesse hated that Brock had to witness this.

"Deputy James didn't pull me over," Jesse said evenly.

Clinton laughed, all his ill humor aimed at Jesse. "Sorry. Looked like she was making you walk the line."

Jesse bristled, wishing he had something to hold in his hands to keep them from fisting. Talking to Clinton any longer was a bad idea. He needed to leave. Pivoting, he caught Brock's eye. His brother-in-law watched him with the rest of the store, but unlike the others, Brock was tensed, like he was ready to ditch the checkout line and come to Jesse's aid.

That fortified Jesse's determination to avoid conflict. Brock and Josie didn't need Clinton's ill intentions focused on them.

But Clinton dogged his heels. "My old man says you're Caleb Cruise's hired hand."

"Yup." Jesse found the racks of oil and dragged his gaze around until he found generic supplies. He skipped over the oil pans and funnels until he found bins lined next to each other.

"You think it's a good idea to hang around Moore?"

Ten, nine, eight, seven...*I'm calm, I'm collected, I'm irritated as fuck.*

Jesse grabbed a plug from each bin instead of taking the

time to find the right one. That'd only give Clinton extra time to dog him.

"I don't hang around Moore," Jesse said, hightailing it for the checkout. He was being prudent; he wasn't a coward. He might have to change his mantra to that the rest of the night. "I work at Caleb's."

"Farah lives next to him. Heard she was your jailer."

Everyone in the store was staring at them. A "fuck" hovered on his lips when he saw the checkout line was four people deep. Brock had just gotten to the counter. He tipped his head to the pile of his items. Sweet. Jesse could add his to Brock's and leave.

"Yeah, she was." What else could Jesse say? The way people watched him as he stalked up to Brock and laid his plugs on the counter made him wonder if his tattoos were glowing. It was a small town, but tattoos weren't unusual. But felons with arms full of tattoos in their auto-parts store was.

Clinton leaned against the counter next to him, his body angled out and his face turned toward him like they were chatting at the bar. "I don't know if I like someone like you living so close to her."

Before Jesse could stop himself, the words left his mouth. "Afraid I'm going to record her most private moments?"

The large man running the cash register made a choking sound, a cross between a laugh and a *holy shit I can't believe you went there*. Jesse calmly handed a twenty to Brock to pay for his stuff.

Red infused Clinton's face. He was the quintessential high school big shot who'd grown into an adult bully. Prison had been full of guys like him. Jesse should run out of the store as fast as he could, but experience told him meekness wouldn't help. Standing his ground promised retribution, but it was best to let the idiot dig himself a hole instead of helping him. If Clinton was determined to start shit, Jesse wasn't giving him any fuel. Now, more than ever, it was critical to be the epitome of an unruffled ex-convict. Anything more could and would be used against him.

"You think you're funny?" Clinton snarled under his breath.

Jesse looked him in the eye. "That's something I've never been accused of. No, I think Deputy James can take care of herself like she takes care of the rest of the county." The clerk handed a bag to Brock, his wide, disbelieving eyes on Jesse. "Have a nice day," he said to Clinton as he walked away with Brock.

Clinton's soft "Oh, I will" followed him out, hanging in the air like a threat.

~

"1506, THIS IS DISPATCH."

Farah hit the button on her mike. "1506, go ahead."

"Dillon Walker called in. There's an alarm going off at his residence. He wasn't home at the time, but he's en route."

"On my way." Farah clicked off and found the nearest approach on the dirt road she was on. She turned around and spun out, gravel flying behind her. Hitting the lights, she accelerated to a speed that was slow enough to keep her from fishtailing out of control.

She didn't bother with the sirens. No one was around. The highway approached and she cleared it to the other side, turning toward town. Taking the first right, she aimed straight for Dillon's.

The Walker side of town was usually pretty quiet. But since Dillon's trouble with Jesse, they'd all amped up security. Was it a malfunction?

Her stomach sank. Smoke rippled above the trees around Dillon's house. A fire?

"Please be a massive family grill-out." It wouldn't be unusual for the Walkers.

She turned down the driveway. There were enough vehicles to have a party, but the guys lining the outside of the shop, each with either a hose or a fire extinguisher in hand, weren't having a good time. Clouds of smoke billowed from what had to have been a former blaze in the back corner of the building. The darkest, most concealed spot in the yard.

Fuck.

She let dispatch know she'd arrived and asked if fire had been called. Nope. If Dillon hadn't called, then he must feel it wasn't necessary. A quick scan of the new and smoldering shop and the rest of the yard didn't reveal any further danger.

A fire. In Dillon's shop.

"What's going on?" Her nose twitched from the smoke. Water puddled at the outer corner of the shop and her boots splattered against the wet pavement pad in front of the building.

The guys finally noticed her. The sun was setting, the light in the sky fading, but she easily made out the five cousins that made up the Walker Five, as well as Justin Walker, Travis's brother.

"Someone started a fire," Dillon growled. He was squatting at the singed corner with a black Maglite flashlight trained on the spot in question.

Someone opened the large overhead door and flooded the area with lights. Much better. She stayed with Dillon. The light cast shadows over his grim features, the blue of his irises nearly glowing with repressed rage.

She glanced around. She wasn't a fire expert, but the

metal construction of the shop had likely saved it from total destruction.

Dillon rose, towering over her, his jaw muscle jumping. "We were all at Travis's when my phone buzzed with an alarm. I flew home to find my damn shop on fire. *Again.*"

Most of the foam from the extinguishers had been washed away by the hoses, but the focal point of the fire was clear. Someone had piled tinder by the back corner and lit it up.

"Do you have video?" she asked.

"Damn right I do." He pulled out his phone and brought up the image. It was grainy and dark. The camera didn't have the best range, but Dillon had managed to catch every inch of his yard, no matter how obscure. After what Jesse had put him through, she couldn't blame him.

And she couldn't believe that her Jesse had done that.

And she couldn't believe she just thought of him as *her* Jesse. She'd forced him out of her mind since the kiss.

Dillon ran through various time points, but the only portion of interest was a dark, crouched form the size and build of a man darting from the tree rows to the shop. The bulky bag he had on his back looked like a black backpack.

Her stomach clenched. Looked suspicious. She glanced at Dillon's face. He was holding his anger in well.

"I want this fucker found." His voice shook, but the hand holding the phone was rock solid.

She dreaded her next question, but she had to ask. "Do you know of anyone who'd want to do this to you?"

The muscle jumped in his jaw again. She expected the fury in his eyes, but the confusion mixed in was a surprise. "I'm not one to dredge up the past, but we all know who comes to mind, especially with him staying only miles away."

She didn't have to ask who Dillon was referring to. He opened his mouth, closed it. Uncertainty passed through his gaze, but he gave his head a firm shake. "Look. If he's innocent, it should be easy to determine it wasn't him, right?"

Not always. The image was unclear and Jesse had his past. If it wasn't Jesse, and they couldn't find the real perpetrator, the cloud of suspicion and doubt would hang over Jesse. But…Dillon didn't seem ready to demand a manhunt for Jesse.

"Do you want to file a report?" She hoped Dillon remembered what that entailed. Jesse would be the prime suspect—guilty or innocent.

"I…want to get who did this."

She chewed on her inner lip, knowing what she was about to suggest was riding the line of professionalism. But for some reason, Dillon wasn't calling for Jesse's head. "I'll talk to Jesse Rodriguez, or at least see if he's willing to talk. Just to cover our bases, is there anyone you can think of who'd want to make it look like Rodriguez was the one who did this?"

Dillon's brows crashed down. Yeah. She was just as clueless as he was. The Walkers didn't have enemies. They were well liked, respected, and always willing to help out. They worked so diligently for what they had, it was hard to be jealous of their success.

A shadow approached. Farah tensed, her hand raising over her weapon. A hazard of her work. She was on the job, therefore she always had to be ready.

It was Brock, his face lined with concern, his hands jammed into his jean pockets. His clothing was drenched from manning a leaky garden hose. "What am I going to tell Josie?"

"Nothing, yet. I'd rather talk to Jesse before anyone else has a chance to." A person's reaction to news told her a lot. And since she was so damn attuned to Jesse, it'd help or hurt him in this case. "Speaking of which, did he know you were all going to be gone tonight?"

Please say no. She'd seen enough of a distraught Josie when she'd visited Jesse in jail. Farah had no wish to pop up on the girl's doorstep, asking about what she'd told her brother.

"I talked to him in town this morning. He was planning to come over, but I told him where we'd be."

Her lips flattened. Jesse couldn't catch a break. He shouldn't, if he was guilty.

"I don't… If it was Jesse, I don't get it." Dillon shook his head again. "He's been sending me money."

"What?" Farah cocked her head like she needed to hear better.

Everyone focused on them. The rest of the Walkers approached.

Dillon scowled at the burn spot in the grass. "While he was in prison, he wrote us both a letter, me and Elle. It was an explanation and an apology. He said he planned to pay everything back though he knew it'd take years. Said he couldn't promise a set amount until he was back on his feet, but he had to do it. And"—Dillon's gaze flicked to Brock—"he asked me to keep the info from Josie. He was worried she'd try to send money in his name, and she'd taken enough responsibility for him."

Jesse was sending Dillon money? Hope surged. Had she really thought it was him?

Cash stepped forward. Times like this, her small stature was painfully obvious. Not one of these guys was under six feet.

"Let's pretend the guy is innocent." Cash's expression said he wasn't buying it, but Dillon's confession had planted doubt in his mind. "Would someone do this to mess with Dillon, or to mess with Jesse?"

They all fell quiet.

Silence would do nothing to help her do her job, or find out if Jesse was innocent or guilty. "Dillon, do you plan to file a report?"

He sighed and glanced at Brock. "I guess I have to. I want this shit to stop no matter who it is, but I can't put Josie through that. Can I make a report without this blowing up on us?"

"It won't be a manhunt if that's what you're asking. If he can clear himself, then we keep looking for who did it." Farah tallied her list of things to do before she left the scene. "I'll wrap up here and go find him."

CHAPTER 7

$\mathcal{H}$eadlights from outside flared into the dim living room. Jesse ripped his attention off an old rerun of *Cold Case* he hadn't seen before and sat up, wincing at the tenderness of his shoulders. He should've kept his shirt on while mowing.

Who was here? Caleb wasn't off duty until morning and it was nearly midnight. Whoever was here was parking in the back and swinging around to face out. Were they going to stop or was it a wrong turn?

He padded into the kitchen to peek out the window. Stepping to the side, he stayed hidden as he peered outside.

A patrol car.

Farah?

Three sharp knocks resounded on the back door.

He couldn't be thrilled to see her. She wouldn't stop by on or off duty for fun in her work vehicle.

Just in case it was another deputy, he checked under the yellowed curtain on the back door. It was Farah and from her stony face, no, she wasn't here for fun.

He opened the door. "Deputy James."

Her eyes widened on his bare chest before she jerked her gaze up to meet his eyes. "Jesse. Can I come in?"

As if he could ever turn her away, uniform or not. He walked away and went straight to the living room. Silence descended after he flicked the TV off, amplifying his heart pounding in his ears.

God, he didn't want to go back to prison, or the small jail of Moore. Farah in full ensemble set his nerves on edge. He perched on the end of the couch. Why was she here? What if something horrible had happened?

His heart threatened to explode. "Is Josie all right?"

"Yes. I'm not here because someone got hurt."

"Oh. Good." He pressed his fingertips together. The remains of his supper from earlier—Hot Pockets, with a chaser of Toaster Strudels—was still on the end table. And he hadn't showered once he'd finished push mowing the dandelions that threatened to take over the yard. He had only moved from the couch to prepare his food.

If he had known he was getting company, he would've done more tonight than enjoy the tiny AC unit chugging along in the living room window. Maybe he should've put a shirt on, but his male ego liked how her eyes kept straying to his chest. And his shoulders were dry and tight from the sun beating down. He should've stopped for a bottle of sunscreen before he left town.

Farah rubbed a temple, her gaze boring a hole in the worn shag carpet. She lifted her head to meet his eyes. "Look, I'll come right out and ask where you were all evening."

His brows lifted. Something had happened, but no one was injured. Yet it didn't sound good for him. "I've been here."

"Anyone who can vouch for you?"

He looked around. The only sounds besides their voices were the creaks of the floor when Farah shifted her weight.

Her mouth tightened. "Anyone who can confirm you've been here all night?"

"The hooker I sent home a half hour ago," he said sarcastically. Alarm flashed in Farah's eyes. Small satisfaction. "No. I've been alone. I walked a few miles mowing the damn lawn, then I changed the oil in the riding lawn mower after cutting out that damn oil drain plug." The incident at the auto-parts store welled in his mind, spiking his ire. To work off his frustration and deter any thoughts of revenge, he'd push mowed the lawn as soon as he'd gotten back. "After that, I made myself a four-course meal: two Hot Pockets and then two toaster pastries. It was a long day in the heat."

His plans to buy a grill and steaks and eat something that had a chance of sticking to his ribs had died after his run-in with Clinton.

She considered him for a moment. He was dying to demand what was going on, but it'd only make him seem hostile.

"There was a fire at Dillon Walker's," she said flatly.

That was not what he'd expected to hear.

"Fuck." Jesse closed his eyes and buried his head in one hand, his elbows propped on his thighs. And Farah was here asking him about it. So many implications. "You said no one was hurt?"

"Just his shop."

Jesse's shoulders sagged. That fucking shop. "And since you're here, it wasn't an accident and they think I did it."

Betrayal ate at him. They had no reason not to think it wasn't him, but he was trying to make amends. Look where it had gotten him.

She shifted, her gear creaking with her movements. A sigh left her, and he dropped his hand to stare up at her.

"Actually, not really. Your name came up, of course, but Dillon told me about the letters and the money."

Jesse clenched his jaw. That was supposed to be his shame to own. He didn't want input from others on what he should or shouldn't do, or for people to ask why bother, since he'd done his time. Nothing was enough to make up for what he'd done.

"Does Josie know?"

"By now she might."

Jesse's phone vibrated on the table at the end of the couch. The piece was so rickety, the vibration might shake it apart. This whole house was a shithole, but it was well lived in and the love through the decades resonated in the walls. If he were to get sentimental and shit, he would say it reminded him of the house he'd lived in when his dad was alive. He didn't want to leave.

"Go ahead and tell her you'll call back." Farah's sincerity gave him hope, which was a wicked bitch. He'd been living off hope of a brighter future for two weeks and here he was, getting interrogated by a cop he'd rather date.

He snagged his phone, punched in a message that he'd call her back, and tossed it down.

"So what now?" he asked.

"I need to ask you some questions." Her keen gaze scanned the room. "And I'd like to have a look around."

He lifted a brow. "Shouldn't you have a warrant?"

"How official do you want me to be?" She swallowed, the action belying her hard-ass routine. "I'd rather be able to report that you let me have a look around and I didn't find anything."

He chuckled with more than a little scorn. "You want to know the fucked-up thing? I ate like a college freshman tonight because I didn't dare buy a grill, or coals, and especially not a lighter or so much as a book of matches after running into Clinton at the store today. So go ahead. You're not going to find anything around here that started that fire."

Her gaze sharpened. "You ran into Clinton? What happened?"

He told her everything. Her mouth twitched at his comment about her protecting the county. A thought dawned on him. It was too much of a coincidence to ignore.

"Clinton was also there when Brock told me the Walkers were meeting at Travis's tonight."

She didn't reply, but her emotions etched into the poker face she wore when she was in uniform. Understanding. Anger. Determination.

"Huh" was all she said before turning to walk out the door. "Come with me."

He stuffed his feet into his boots at the door and followed her outside. "What are we doing?"

She retrieved a black flashlight from her belt and shone it on a spot in front of his pickup. "Stand over there while I check this quick."

He couldn't pretend to like the outcome of the evening, but he trusted Farah not to screw him over. They didn't know each other well, but the first thing he'd learned about her was that she was a stickler for doing her job properly.

It was a miracle his lips had been allowed to touch hers. He knew it never would've happened when she was in uniform. Swaying to his right, he fought to catch a view of her rounded ass poking out of the pickup. There wasn't much to look through. The cubbies inside were empty and aside from dirty rags and receipts she was probably inspecting, Jesse hadn't driven it enough to fill it with junk. None of his vehicles were ever filled with garbage. He stored the receipts inside to turn into Caleb and the rags were often needed for a last minute *oh shit I have grease on my face* wipe.

Farah stepped back and shut the door. She swiped her flashlight across the body of pickup to dip inside the box, then underneath.

"Walk with me through the out buildings."

Again, she found nothing. The place she concentrated on most was the garage where he did the majority of his work.

"Why'd you use the push mower?" The light in the garage had as much power as twenty fireflies, but Farah shut her flashlight off.

Because he'd been pissed. "I wanted to make sure I got it done. I couldn't promise the tractor would start after I got the oil changed and put fresh gas in it. Turns out, it was a good thing. It won't turn over."

"You've given yourself a hell of a sunburn."

He glanced at his right shoulder and grimaced. Redness bloomed across his skin. It hadn't been that bad when he'd quit for the night.

"Do you have any ointment?" At his blank look, she kept going. "Aloe? Aspirin? Oatmeal?"

"Other than the aloe, how does any of that help a sunburn?"

She ignored his question. "Baking soda?"

"Neither Caleb nor I have baked any cookies lately."

"For the burn. They're home remedies. Never mind. I'm done with my shift soon. I'll pick something up and bring it over."

"You came here to arrest me, but you're treating my owies?" He went for stern and sardonic, but the warm fuzzies her concern gave him probably made him look like a needy stray puppy.

She gave him a bored look. "Happens more than you'd think. Want my help or not? Before you answer, I'd like to look around your room."

He returned her look with a placid expression. "Yes. I want you to run errands for me *because* you're searching my belongings for evidence."

"Lead the way then and I'll find aloe gel for you."

Cooling ointment for the fire currently smoldering along his shoulders sounded divine.

He led her back to the house and up the stairs to the tiny bedroom on the right. Caleb's room was the larger one behind the living room, with the full bath between them. Jesse had a square bathroom he could stand upright in, unlike the bedroom. In his room, the ceiling slanted at a steep angle and once he crossed the threshold, he had to start ducking or get severe lacerations from the popcorn ceiling.

"Oh my God, nothing's changed," Farah breathed as she looked around, standing fully upright. "I remember when Grandma Cruise made that quilt." She stroked her hand across the blanket draped over his bed. "These are Caleb's grandpa's old work shirts. That woman never threw anything away."

Jesse had guessed that from his short time living in the house. He didn't say anything. Watching Farah fondle the quilt was enough entertainment for him.

She snatched her hand back like she'd remembered her reason for being in his room. He doubted he was supposed to be in here while she looked, so he leaned against the door-jamb. What did she think she'd have to look through? He had nothing more than a couple changes of clothes and a charging cable for his phone. His wallet was in his pocket and that summed up all his things. Josie and Brock had stored his remaining few possessions.

Farah zeroed in on his backpack. It lay on the floor next to the four-drawer dresser that weighed as much as he did. She hefted it, dug around inside, and pulled out his only prize possession.

A photo album. He almost stepped forward to snatch it out of her hands, but he crossed his arms instead.

"Want to blackmail me with awkward family photos,

you're holding all the power right there," he said, forcing the words past the lump in his throat.

He'd carried that thing with him everywhere he'd lived since getting out of prison, but he hadn't looked through it once since.

What would Ma have thought about what he'd done?

Farah opened the cover, then her hand stalled. She closed it and shoved it back in the pack. And sniffed it.

He snorted, earning a glare from her.

"The perpetrator wore a black backpack. I'm smelling for accelerant or smoke."

Because that was Jesse's shitty luck. "I should've bought the neon-pink one with unicorns."

Her mouth quirked. "That would be more your style."

He laughed, the stress of the situation lessening. It'd never be gone completely. He hadn't allowed himself to even think about the woman for the last three years because of the naughty fantasies she inspired, and she was investigating him for something he couldn't prove he hadn't done.

Dropping the backpack, she gave him a regretful smile. "I'm done here. I need to wrap up my shift and get the reports done. Then I'll stop back with some medicine."

"What about charges and the fire and who did it?"

Her smile faded. "I'm still looking into it."

She swept past him and down the stairs. Before she plowed out the back door, she stopped and looked back.

And that was that. He was alone again.

Anger bubbled under his skin. Had Clinton dragged Dillon and his family into this sick shit he was playing? Had he done it to get back at Jesse for being a smartass?

Fuck. He cocked a fist to nail the wall. But it wasn't his wall and he couldn't waste time or money on repairing drywall. Or risk his job because Caleb learned he had anger management issues.

Jesse balled his fists and prowled the top floor. There wasn't a damn thing he could do. Being stupid and charging over to Clinton's sprawling property would land him in jail. Not to mention what he'd do to the guy based on his past history with Farah.

His skin felt constricting around him and it had nothing to do with the sunburn. He wanted to crawl outside of himself. Farah had to investigate him.

He'd come here to help his sister and been nothing but trouble for her since.

He squeezed his fists. It wasn't enough. A snarl ripped out of his mouth. He dropped and banged out a push-up, then jumped up. Jumping jack. One burpee down. Not bothering to keep count, he kept on until his muscles quivered with each flex. His sides heaved, his lungs burned, and the burn on his back and shoulders screamed like his skin was going to split apart.

But his rage died down, like the old-timer in the prison had claimed it would. He'd seen a protégée in Jesse, someone who could either leave prison early based on good behavior or a guy who'd spend the rest of his life inside, constantly fucking up.

Expend the negative energy.

Jesse couldn't think about what would happen if he committed death by burpees. He needed more than a count-down to get him through tonight and he clung to the one-day-at-a-time mentality. Sweat trickled down his forehead and he almost slammed his face into the threadbare orange carpet. Five more burpees and he'd go shower, once he was sure he'd be mellow Jesse when Farah showed again.

Why the hell was a two-ounce bottle of aloe gel eight dollars? It was almost as expensive as the tiny spray bottle of sunscreen she'd chosen. What a racket. Convenience shouldn't cost that much.

Farah grabbed a couple packs each of the painkillers the gas station carried. *I'm grumbling like Dad.*

But it was after two in the morning and she was willing to pay more to not have to enter the big box store that was open all night.

Her shift had slipped away as she wrapped up the paperwork on Dillon's case. She'd worked a few hours extra, but that wasn't unusual and half of it had been searching Jesse's minimal items.

Was that all the guy had to his name?

Maybe his sister was storing more for him. With no place to call his own, she must be hanging on to it.

Farah had found nothing to incriminate him. In the morning she'd ask her parents if they noticed Jesse out mowing at any time yesterday. They might not be able to definitively prove it wasn't Jesse, but the more doubt they cast his way, the better his life in Moore would be.

What if he packed his one backpack and took off?

Farah stalled at the end of the aisle. Did she really think Jesse would leave?

Did she really think he'd willingly endure hostile treatment in a random store and accusations of criminal activity?

She dropped her items on the counter.

The older woman working the night shift smiled with tired eyes. "Hey, Farah. Busy night?"

"Oh, you know. Same old, same old." It was Farah's standard reply and seemed to mollify people. Some dug for gossip, others genuinely cared, but Farah didn't have the mental energy to determine each person's motivation. Gladys probably greeted every policeman, deputy, and highway patrolman the same, including other emergency personnel.

Gladys chuckled. "Isn't that the truth." She rang up the items. "I'll never get over my sense of déjà vu seeing you walk in. Your mom used to the do same thing. Except maybe to get the aloe gel. How's your mama doing?"

Sadness rang through Farah. She loved her job, but she never wanted to reach a point where she chewed painkillers from the effects of the stress of this work. Mom hadn't dealt with it well. Her position as sheriff had not only come with heaps of responsibility, but also with being the figurehead for the whole department. And Mom being Mom, she'd refused to stay office-bound and had taken turns patrolling the county. But the stroke had wiped all those items from her agenda. Now her recovery spread the stress between her, Dad, and Farah.

Still, she stuck to saying nothing more than what people could assume from seeing her parents around town. "Mom's good. She's walking with a cane and her speech is much clearer than a few months ago." She handed a twenty over.

"Good. That's good." Gladys finished ringing her up and dropped the change in Farah's hand. "Tell her I miss her. That woman needs to concentrate on herself now. The degenerates that gave her a hard time aren't her problem anymore."

No, now they were Farah's.

Fatigue weighed on her. She'd normally be in bed by now, popping up at dawn to help Dad with the livestock. She could sneak in a couple more hours of sleep in the morning, but Dad never had a day off and he wasn't getting any younger. He needed her help.

But first, she needed to drop these off with Jesse.

She drove out of town toward her home. Passing Jesse's, she made the last-minute decision to change first. Showing up again in her uniform and patrol car didn't sit well with her after earlier. And she tried to keep a clear distinction between personal and professional errands, not using her work car on her own time. Same with the clothing. The aloe gel was a minor exception. Minor.

She drove into her yard. It was larger than Caleb's. Her parents had expanded over the years while Caleb's family had been content to keep their operation small. A small godsend. He couldn't keep a larger operation alive, while Farah would have to make the decision whether to walk away from it all and sell the place once Dad passed away. If they could make it that long. His advancing age had been a disadvantage even before Mom's stroke, but now...

Parking in front of the shop that housed the mother-in-law suite she lived in, she shook off her worries. She wasn't going to get into bed any earlier by sitting in her car chewing on problems that had bugged her all day.

Inside, she changed, choosing black yoga pants and a light

T-shirt. The night temperatures didn't dip below sixty this time of year and when the sun went down, it was sometimes the only part of the day the wind didn't hound them.

Back outside with flip-flops to replace her boots, she frowned at her choice of wheels. Maybe this wasn't a good idea. Why didn't she just drop the bag off with Jesse and get home to crawl into bed?

She finger-combed her hair. That should've been left in its bun, too. She probably had a wicked indent in her hairline from the tie. It draped over her shoulders, long enough to tie back without a million flyaway strands.

There was a path through the trees to Caleb's but she'd never crossed it in the dark. The yard lights and a flashlight would help, but she couldn't risk twisting an ankle. Okay, she'd take Mom's car. It was the quietest and she could start it in the garage and muffle the worst of the noise.

If she'd ever been the type of teenager to sneak out, she would've died from the adrenaline. The fear of waking her parents and explaining herself was going to give her a heart attack. This was nothing like a high-speed chase on narrow county highways.

She didn't flip her headlights on until she'd cleared her house, and it only took a minute to get to Caleb's place.

She parked facing out, a habit from work she didn't bother to break on her personal time. Tapping on the door, she waited.

Nothing. Dammit, had he fallen asleep?

Why wouldn't he? It was nearing three a.m.

She tested the handle. The door was still unlocked. Letting herself inside, she quietly called for Jesse. No answer. The light over the stairs was on, but it was always on. It'd been the Cruises' nightlight for as long as she remembered. Peeking around the first floor, she didn't find Jesse sleeping on the couch or in the bathroom.

He must be in bed.

Had he not believed she'd bring him supplies?

She should drop her bag on the counter and leave. But she grabbed a glass of water and toed up the stairs, leaving her flip-flops at the bottom.

"Jesse?" Was sneaking up on an ex-convict while he was sleeping a smart idea?

She rounded his doorway, hearing the steady breathing before she laid eyes on him.

Her lips parted. He was sprawled across the quilt she'd admired earlier, fast asleep. As if seeing his chest then hadn't been fodder for fantasies she didn't know she had, this was worse. He was still shirtless, but his jeans were folded neatly on top of his dresser and a towel was wrapped around his waist instead.

It was one thing to know that he must have a rock-hard body underneath that orange jumpsuit, not to mention the muscles that could cut glass she'd seen a couple weeks ago. But now they were all on display. All of them. From rippled abs that cascaded into a trim waist to the strong thighs beneath, it was all on display.

She swallowed and tried to peel her gaze off him, but her eyes kept wandering back. A pair of basketball shorts rested on the blanket next to his hand. He must've showered and fallen asleep before he could dress.

A smile tickled her lips. At times he radiated danger, though it'd been repressed since he'd been back. But here was a guy who was wiped and passed out before he could even dress.

Her gaze swept his form again, lingering on his ink. The tattoos on both arms reached his shoulders. The tribal one wrapped around his bicep like she wanted to, and his other arm was a myriad of different images, the most apparent a fishing boat. What an odd choice. The ink on both sides was black and stark against his brown skin, stopping at his shoulders where the angry red sunburn had set in.

She winced. He was going to peel worse than a garter snake shedding its skin.

The thought finally reminded her that she wasn't here to admire his nudity like a creeper peeking through his window.

"Jesse," she called.

He frowned. Sleep softened his face, making him nearly adorable. Her rugged, tough mechanic actually had cheeks that would give him a baby face if he weren't so lean. The sides of his hair were only an inch long, but a shock of black rested on his forehead. She hadn't seen him completely without a cap, hadn't realized how much of his face it shadowed.

"Jesse," she said louder.

His eyes popped opened and he sat up, scanning the room. They widened when they landed on her before his lips screwed up and he palpated his shoulder.

"Fuck, that hurts." He blinked. "Aw, shit. I fell asleep. Sorry."

He was avoiding her gaze. He'd swung his legs down, one hand propped behind him, while he touched his skin like he was afraid he'd lost a few layers. His position twisted his body enough to define every muscle in his torso. She was going to drool if she kept standing here.

She handed him the water. "I brought some painkillers."

"Right. I looked it up. To rub on it, right?"

She grinned at his sleep-roughened voice. He'd done what she said. "You can, but I bought aloe gel for that. Here's some ibuprofen."

While he ripped open the packet and downed the pills, she pulled out the sunscreen and set it on the nightstand.

"You might want to keep your shirt on next time, but just

in case, I picked this up." She smirked. "You might have to risk a farmer's tan."

"I thought I was ranching."

"But the tan lines are the same."

He scowled at his darker arms, comparing it to the lighter bronze skin of his abdomen. The thin blue towel had managed to stay closed around his waist.

She handed him the gel. "Put this on now and again in the morning. Do it a few times a day to keep the pain down."

He stretched to set the empty water glass on the night-stand. She jerked her gaze to the ceiling instead of letting it fall on the crease of the towel. Was it gaping open?

The bottle was lifted out of her hand. "Thanks," he said gruffly. "You must be tired."

"It's the waking up that sucks. I need to get up early and help Dad."

Jesse lifted a brow as he squirted green goo into one palm. "That's only a couple hours away. Your dad is out there at the ass crack of dawn."

She shrugged. Why wasn't she heading out the door right now? "He might wait and let me catch a few more winks."

Jesse massaged the gel into one shoulder and groaned. "It hurts so good."

She was about to pivot and careen down the stairs after being way too comfortable with a naked Jesse, but seeing him rub down his shoulders brought another question to mind. "How bad is your back?"

"I'm afraid to look. My shoulders are the worst."

Before she could list all the reasons why she should leave, just leave, she snatched the bottle out of his hand and walked around the bed.

The broad expanse of his back was marred by the stria-tions the blanket had made while he slept, but there was just as much redness down the middle swatch as there was on his shoulders.

"Oh my God, Jesse. You really did a number on yourself." Concern propelled her to kneel on the quilt and crawl over to him.

His shoulders tensed and he glanced at her, his dark gaze incredulous. "That bad? Getting too much sun isn't something I normally worry about when I'm working under the hood."

His tone had dropped a few notches. She squirted cool gel into her hands, rubbed them together, then spread them across his back.

He jerked, then moaned and relaxed into her touch. They both stayed silent as she massaged wherever it was red. She worked up his hard back to his broad shoulders.

This was a bad idea. The more she touched his heated skin, the harder it was to quit doing it. He rolled his head with her movements, releasing a pleased groan. She liked eliciting that reaction from him. She liked what it did to her, how the sound traveled through her body, igniting desire in its wake.

"I should go," she whispered, her hands resting on his back.

He twisted around under her hands to look at her. "I know." He'd said that before. And she knew he truly understood. And accepted. If he hadn't, he would've been resistible. But he got her, knew her work was important to her despite not knowing all her personal reasons why. Like how she needed the benefits, how her work floated their ranch because Dad couldn't work as many cattle as he used to, or how she'd only ever dreamed of being in law enforcement like her mother and if she lost it, she'd have to start from square one with her identity.

She tipped her forehead to his and turned on her knees until they were almost side by side. "Jesse."

She kissed him this time and it flipped open the latch on his restraint like she'd opened the cattle gate and burst through. He wrapped an arm around her waist and surged over her. She landed on her back, with him over her, their lips smashed together.

Opening for him, she darted her tongue out and was instantly welcomed by his. She'd instinctively widened her legs to allow him to settle between them. His erection pressed into her, hot and hard and pushing past the towel. The towel had failed at its job as soon as he'd moved.

She dug her hands into his glossy hair. It was as soft as she'd imagined and she'd been lying to herself about how often she'd dreamed of doing this.

He had been anchoring himself on his hands over her, but he gave up more of his weight over her. She moaned into his mouth. Yes. More.

The need inside of her raged too strong. She rocked her hips into him, trying to position his shaft to push against the spot that needed it the most. Her hands drifted from his hair to around his back.

He jerked and she pulled her mouth away. "Oh God, I'm so sorry."

"Fucking worth it." He kissed down her neck to nibble over her pulse. She shuddered into him and tightened her legs around him.

"I need—" She needed to get off really bad, but she was too timid to say it.

He lifted his head to smile down at her, his eyes full of wicked promise. "I know." He tunneled one hand under her waistband. Her decision to dress in yoga pants was the best one she'd made all day.

When his rough fingertips grazed her clit, she jackknifed

her back off the mattress. It'd been so long since she'd taken care of own needs, much less had anyone else do it for her.

She'd been wet and ready for him since she'd seen him without a shirt—way before that, actually—but not like this. His smooth circles around her nub were going to do the job, but she was still restless. She needed more. "I want you inside me," she said, kicking her pelvis up to prove a point.

He lifted his head from her neck, his expression a mass of confusion like he hadn't heard her correctly. It changed to full dismay. "I…don't have any protection."

She went still, cursing her lack of preparation. "Nothing? What have you been using?"

"I haven't needed them. Not since before—" He pressed his lips shut like he didn't want to bring up the elephant parked between them. "I didn't want the kind of women who were attracted to a man on probation. And I was on probation for four years, so…"

A man like him wasn't someone she'd associate abstinence with.

"I haven't for a long time either."

He looked pleased at her revelation. She knew how he felt.

He rocked forward, his body putting pressure on where his hand rested against her.

Her eyelids fluttered. The pleasure pushed her closer to a climax.

"I wanted you the first time I saw you," he admitted.

She paused again and met his eyes. His confession was heartfelt and not something he'd said to keep them from stopping. She was compelled to make an admission of her own.

"You—you get me. And it's intoxicating."

He leaned down to whisper in her ear at the same time he

resumed stroking her clit. "Because none of the guys here are man enough for you, Deputy James."

Oh God. He had to go there. A thrill speared her and she bucked against him. He adjusted his hold to curl his free arm under her while he slid one long finger down her slit. When he pushed inside of her, she whimpered and tilted into him.

She almost dug her nails into his back. No, she couldn't hurt him again. She wedged her arm between them and grabbed his shaft.

He let out a ragged groan and trembled in her arms. They moved together, his thumb rubbing circles while her hand fisted his cock and his finger stroked in and out.

The climax crashed into her. She tightened around him and cried out, her reaction setting him off. Hot fluid coated her hand and his body shook in her arms. He stroked her as she rode out her orgasm. His hot breath tickled her ear, sending shivers down her spine.

When they were spent, he shifted to use the towel to clean them up. She was boneless as he set it aside and curled her into him. He kept the majority of his sunburn off the bed as he surrounded her. She was asleep before she could remind herself this was a bad idea.

CHAPTER 9

*V*ibrating roused Jesse. He clicked his phone off and the alarm he'd set after Farah had fallen asleep. He lifted himself on an elbow to watch the woman in his arms.

The halo of pale hair around Farah's head was so unlike the stern jailer he'd first met. Sleep wasn't the only thing that softened her. Being out of her uniform changed her personality.

But he liked each facet she revealed. He wouldn't have trusted another deputy to search his room. He was too easy of an answer, but not for her.

"Farah." He caressed her cheek. She frowned in her sleep but turned into him. If he could have his way, he'd wrap them both in the quilt and sleep all morning while the birds sang outside the window. Then when they woke, he would bring her pleasure again.

But she'd mentioned helping her dad, and she'd never forgive herself if she slept in and left her dad to carry the burden alone.

"Farah, it's seven in the morning."

Her eyes sluggishly blinked open. She'd barely gotten three hours of sleep and had to be supremely tired. "Seven?" she mumbled.

"Sorry, I wanted to let you sleep, but Caleb is coming home soon and you said you wanted to help with chores."

She sucked in a breath and sat up. "Oh shit. I've never been gone from home all night when I wasn't working."

"Never?" Sure, she'd said she hadn't dated, and like him, she hadn't been prepared to bypass the dinners and drinks straight to sex, but… Never?

She rubbed her eyes and yawned. "Well, except for college and the police academy, but no, I haven't dated and I haven't ventured out of the county for a hookup."

He caught himself grinning but hid it. Farah James liked him. It wasn't his bad-boy status or the allure of the forbidden. She hadn't seemed like the type, but having it confirmed assuaged his ego.

She caught him smiling. "You said you haven't…you know."

"Fucked anyone since I got out of prison? Correct." He peered at her. Her cheeks pinked. "Holy crap, are you blushing?"

Shoving his shoulder, she scowled at him, but he caught her hand and kissed her wrist.

"I made Deputy James blush." Her scowl deepened closer to a what-have-I-done look. He elaborated on their conversation. "After meeting you, most other girls I crossed paths with were as…ordinary as an oil change. I told you my girlfriend dumped me after Bill screwed me over. It upset me, but truth was, the few long-term relationships I've had were mostly superficial. I had nothing to give them and I was worried about myself. But I met you and—"

She arched a light brow. "And you worried about me. The girl cop around all the bad men?"

He barked out a laugh. "No. I realized that there are self-sufficient women out there who I don't have to worry about. My other relationships, they all wanted something out of me, demanded a lifestyle I wasn't ready to give. But you had your school, had a job, and put up with zero shit. I haven't met another woman like you." He hadn't looked. "But I'm gonna worry about you because people are stupid and it's your job to protect the public from them."

She looked away and sighed. "I don't know if I can keep seeing you. I want to. But we shouldn't."

He dropped his gaze to the patterned quilt draped over his lap. He only had himself to blame. Without his crimes he wouldn't have met her, yet because of his crimes he couldn't be with her.

Looking around, she crouched and came up with the bottle of gel. Squirting a glob in her hand, she motioned for him to turn around. It was hard to do so and keep his growing erection covered, but he managed. Her firm touch massaged cooling aloe over his burn. It felt a lot better than last night, but desire smothered all other emotion. The fear that someone was framing him paled against Farah's hands on him. He could lose his job if Caleb came home and caught them in bed together and blamed Jesse for threatening his friend's well-being, yet it was almost a nonissue when he was in the same room with Farah. She wouldn't be intimidated away by Caleb.

If she wanted space from Jesse, she'd make sure it happened.

He unraveled himself from the quilt and stood on the opposite side of the bed. Her gaze tracked him, hooking on his uncomfortably hard shaft. Flipping the covers back, he crawled under them, enjoying the disappointment flitting through her features.

"You'd better get home. If you decide you want to see me

again, give me a call. And maybe stop by with some more of those sandwiches." The bread wasn't a juicy, seared steak, but it was better than the rest of the food under this roof.

She chewed her lip and nodded. "Get some rest."

When she was gone, Jesse dragged in a deep breath and released it slowly. Would he even see her again?

GUILT SEEPED through Jesse as he watched the green countryside fly by. The expanses of emerald pastures were broken up by black fields that had been freshly planted. Glints of blue from stock ponds and small lakes in the horizon twinkled against the fluffy white clouds of the sky.

He should be back helping Caleb, but after he'd rolled out of bed at noon and found Caleb in the barn, Caleb had asked when he'd last taken a day off. "I thought since you were sleeping all day, you'd declared it Jesse's day."

Jesse had meant to only grab a few hours of sleep to keep from hurting himself and being no good to anyone.

"Seriously, Jesse. We all need a break. I heard about last night and I'm sure your sister wants details."

It was Caleb's tone that got him. He wasn't accusatory. So then Jesse bluntly asked his opinion and Caleb just snorted about knowing how long the lawn took to mow and if the back of Jesse's neck was any indication, Jesse hadn't had time to sneak around Moore lighting fires.

So Jesse had spent the whole day with his sister. But not in Moore.

They'd gone to Alexandria to shop. Josie had dragged him through farm and supply stores for durable jeans and boots and shirts. Then they'd swung through a department store so he could buy personal items. It took the skills of a special agent, but he'd snuck away from her long enough to grab a box of condoms and then hidden them as he bought everything. The afternoon brought back echoes of spending the day with her and their mom.

He'd told Josie everything he knew, excluding the part about Clinton but including Farah looking around his place. Otherwise, Josie wouldn't have so easily forgiven him for brushing off her call.

She was the first to break the silence in the car. "You can stay with us, you know. Still work for Caleb, but stay with us." She shot him a sidelong look. "We'll be your alibi and it won't hurt that we're Walkers."

No one would argue with Brock if he declared he'd been with Jesse at the time of a crime. Brock would probably rattle off times down to the minutes.

"No. I'm not guilty." And he'd be farther away from Farah —in case she ignored her best judgment. "And you and Brock are preparing for the baby."

Josie snorted. "It's our first. It's not like I'm juggling other small kids. We buy a crib, put it up, and wait."

Jesse remembered the days he was an only child. Barely, but there were a few. He'd been young when his dad had died, but the few memories he had were good. Dad used to promise to take him fishing when he was older. Those days never came. Jesse had grown, but Dad remained the same age in all of Jesse's memories. And that age was younger than he was now.

What would Dad think of him? Jesse was pushing thirty-four, not exactly homeless but not far removed from sleeping on a friend's couch. His retirement plan was imaginary and his job was temporary at best, and he couldn't see beyond working for Caleb.

"What are you thinking about?" Josie asked. The confines of the car were like a confessional, and Josie had become more than a little sister he had to watch over. She was an equal and a confidant.

"My dad," he said honestly.

"About how different it'd all be?"

He could talk to Josie about a lot, but that his father would label Jesse a loser if he were alive wasn't something he planned to discuss. "About Dad and Grandma. She was so bitter."

"Yeah, she was. I don't remember much about her, except when she'd hold that cigarette, complaining about something." Surprisingly, Grandma had come around after Dad had died and after Ma had remarried.

"The cancer got her before the stuff she complained about did." He didn't remember much more than Josie. Grandma had been estranged from her own parents by then because she'd married Grandpa Rodriguez. His grandpa had been a quiet man, also a heavy smoker, and had died before Grandma.

Like she'd read his mind, Josie said, "Maybe it was for the best they weren't around all the time. With Bill, you didn't need any more negativity."

But it'd been enough to poison his mind. Prison hadn't been the place to work on positive thinking, but it was either that or shank someone.

"How's Bill?" he asked.

Josie lifted a shoulder. "He's afraid of both me and Brock so we don't talk much. For the best."

He watched her. "You have a big family now."

She smiled, but it barely reached her eyes. "Yeah, they're great. Lots of cousins for this little Walker." She patted her belly.

"But."

"But I feel like the ugly duckling sometimes. I go to family functions, I blend, then I come home exhausted. Like that social butterfly isn't me."

"Neither is being surrounded by a large family."

"That's it. I love every one of them. I've never had so much support in my life, but sometimes the stress of being good enough for them wears on me."

Lord knew that feeling had plagued Jesse his whole life. His dad had died on him. His mom had died on him. His grandparents' presence had been lacking even before they died. Bill had used him and basically robbed him blind. Josie was his only family, and he was waiting for her to decide she wasn't worth his time.

Then there was Farah. He didn't have to worry about not being worthy. He wasn't. But he had to help Josie feel better. He'd already failed at the big brother role once. "Maybe they're all worrying about the same thing. I'd say picture them all in their underwear, but Brock probably wouldn't like that."

Josie barked out a laugh. "It'd be a nice picture, but the guys are all like my brothers and their wives are...turning into really good friends."

"You sit around and paint your nails and gossip?"

"Rural Mama Red is the hot color right now. Then we talk about boys and the newest hair styles." Her laughter died. "No, I feel like I can actually talk to them, and growing up in a garage full of men, I haven't had that before."

That explained the fear they'd all shun her eventually. Or pull a Bill and rip the rug out from under her when she needed stability the most.

"They're good people, and good people quit dealing with us when Ma died."

"Ain't that the truth." Josie turned onto the highway that would take them home.

"Doesn't make you not a good person. They wouldn't

have welcomed you into the family if you weren't. In fact, they should be grateful you accepted them."

Josie smiled but changed the subject. "Why didn't you tell me you were paying Dillon back?"

"How much would you have sent him with my name on it?"

She took her gaze off the road long enough to glare at him. "Who said I would?"

"You're not saying you wouldn't. It's my debt to pay, and it'd feel less genuine if I danced through town bragging about how I'm paying him back."

"Would you do the salsa or the mambo through Moore?"

"Isn't it the two-step in this area?"

"Don't knock it. I love Texas two-stepping with Brock."

Jesse chuckled, but his heart flipped. Did Farah dance? He didn't. If they ever got to a point where they dated, would she have to give up dancing, too?

Why was he even thinking that far ahead? She'd told him this morning they were a bad idea.

"Want to come over for supper?" Josie asked. The turnoff to his place was approaching.

"I'd like to, but after last night, I'd better stick to my end of Moore." He'd invite them over, but then he'd have to run to town for food. Caleb had sent him a selfie with the new appliances, but even if the guy had made a food run, Jesse tried to buy his own groceries now that he was getting paid.

"Okay, but call me." She hit the dirt road to his place and they stayed quiet until she pulled into the yard.

Jesse glanced at the time. It was after six. Caleb trotted out of the back door and waved.

Josie rolled down her window and Jesse hopped out. Caleb's hair was slicked back in a swirled style, exposing his shaved sides, and his plugs were in. He wore clean jeans and an Affliction T-shirt.

"Hey, Josie!" Caleb lifted his chin toward Jesse. "Hey, man. I'm going with the guys from work. Everything around here's good."

An engine rumbled down the drive and they all turned. Farah was behind the wheel of a steel-gray Dodge Ram. How many vehicles did her family have?

"Well, the guys and Farah."

Jesse's jaw tensed. He tried to force it to relax but was out of luck. Still standing in the open door of Josie's Mustang, he watched Farah swing around in the drive.

Caleb came around the car and slapped Jesse's shoulder. "You know I'd invite you along, but like I said, it's my work buddies and Farah and a few of the local law enforcement. I don't think it'd be a good time for you."

"I get it. I'm hanging with my sister tonight. It's all good." It wasn't.

Caleb grinned, sympathy in his gaze. He hopped in Farah's truck and they both waved as she left. Farah had barely done more than glance at him, but she'd smiled at Josie.

"Get in," Josie commanded.

He slumped back into the passenger seat, unwilling to be caught in the same position as last night. Alone while some other arsonist was framing him.

Josie turned around and headed to her place. "I didn't know Farah and Caleb were dating."

"They're friends." The reality of his failed infatuation with Farah hit him. It wasn't just his past, or that he couldn't dance. He didn't even know if she did. This was her life. Cops and firemen were her friends. Her mom had been a sheriff. He'd messed up his chances with her long before he'd met her.

CHAPTER 10

"You can't make this shit up," Scotty said as they all laughed about his latest story. He was with the city police and one of the crew that often met to blow off steam and swap war stories. It was one of her favorite nights, one of her only nights out.

Then why'd she feel so crappy?

Was it because Scotty was the one who had arrested Jesse? Or had it been the frustrated and hopeless look on Jesse's face as she'd driven away with Caleb?

She looked around. Their group of eight included her, Caleb, Scotty, four of the firemen he worked with, and another deputy she got along with. Two of the firemen were married, including the only other woman at the table. Max, the other deputy, was also married and twice all of their age, but he was well liked and had always treated her respectfully.

Caleb took a swig from his beer bottle. He was glaring at the door.

"Uh-oh," Farah murmured next to him. Brigit Walker had just walked in with her fiancé. When was Caleb going to get over her? Farah liked all the Walkers, but Brigit had always seemed less friendly and more a cold bitch—and the last person Farah expected Caleb to be hung up on.

Said the deputy who'd woken up with an ex-convict this morning. Farah took a sip of her Coke. It's not as if hormones required a background check.

Brigit's bright eyes skipped over their group, lingering on Caleb. She gave him a nod. It was acknowledgement of her brother's best friend, nothing more, but poor Caleb might read into it.

Caleb lifted a finger from his beer in a wave. "That guy is a walking pile of lying shit," he said quietly to Farah. She'd been his sounding board for his unrequited love for Brigit since high school. It wasn't like he could go to Justin Walker and bitch about his ice princess of a sister.

"But he's dressed for the part," Farah remarked. Brigit's mom had put the kibosh on Brigit dating Caleb, deeming him not good enough for her precious daughter when she should've wept tears of joy that her daughter had fallen for a decent man with a good heart. The man Brigit had hooked up with might look the part, but he oozed seediness.

"Fuck him." Caleb's gaze dropped to the table. "And her, too."

Scotty started in on another story and Caleb leaned in, but Farah would bet her next paycheck that he was still brooding about Brigit.

Poor guy. Farah had always been sympathetic before, but her understanding was suddenly much deeper. She'd liked waking up to a naked Jesse. Liked being by held by him while she slept. Liked hearing that he admired her dedication to her job when it was usually the deal breaker in her meet cutes.

Farah finished her soda and pushed back from the table. They didn't usually stay long past ten p.m., but she wouldn't last the rest of the hour without a bathroom break.

She swept into the bathroom. Blond-haired, stunning, blue-eyed Brigit was at the sink. Farah lifted her brows.

"So, you and Caleb finally, huh?" Brigit said in place of a greeting.

Farah rolled her eyes, a move she rarely indulged in while on duty. "Still friends. Still not sleeping together. Still having to explain that it's possible."

Brigit's mouth twitched. Was she about to smile? Figured Farah would go full bitch while in civilian clothes and still not get taken seriously.

Brigit finished drying her hands. "It was nice to see you again."

Farah blinked as the taller woman breezed out. She'd sounded sincere. Maybe Brigit's icy personality was melting.

She finished in the bathroom and walked to the bar, weaving through tables on her way to order another soda. She should pick a decaf drink, but she was already going nonalcoholic because was driving. Scanning the room, she couldn't help but note who was there, how they were acting, and how much trouble they could cause.

Her stomach sank when she spotted Clinton bending over a pool table. What a surprise. Her Saturday night out and here he was. Again. Last month, he'd been here, too.

He glanced up from his aim, and his eyes narrowed. Tapping the cue against the four ball, he didn't take his gaze off her. She kept her expression blank as she went to the bar.

The bartender popped up from behind the counter, a stack of towels in her hands. "What can I get you, Farah?"

Farah frowned. "Trina. Are you working both the floor and the bar?"

Trina blew a lock of hair out of her face. "Manni's on break. Coke, right?"

Most people assumed Trina was a bitch. She didn't flirt for tips but occasionally dated customers, which wrongly fostered resentment in some clientele because she was discriminatory in who she dated.

Farah recognized Trina's attitude for what it was: she was doing her job and she didn't think she needed to soften her personality to do it. If she did, in her line of work, many men would interpret it incorrectly and think they had a right to pat her ass or ask her out. And many women would dislike her for flirting with all the men.

Trina filled a glass and slid it across. "The guys need anything else?"

Farah glanced at her group. "I'll just get another for Caleb." The others were on a fresh round.

Trina disappeared to grab a bottle of Caleb's brand. A shadow crowded Farah. She tensed, her hand twitching at her side where she usually hooked her Taser. But tonight she only wore jeans and a baby-doll top, armed with nothing more than her wit and her wallet.

Clinton's lips twisted in a smirk as he pinned her under his hooded gaze. "How's it going, Farah?"

Fine until now. "Clinton."

"Is it true Caleb hired that migrant worker?"

Farah choked on her indignation, but the more Clinton riled her, the more power he had. "No, but he hired a guy born and raised in the Land of Ten Thousand Lakes like you and I."

Clinton scoffed and looked around, his gaze lingering on her party. "What's he know about ranching? He looks like he should be in jail."

Blood boiled through her veins, but she remained calm. Mentioning Jesse's jail time would only encourage Clinton. "If we assigned fate by our stereotypes, you'd have issues."

Clinton's blank look lasted a moment before her meaning seeped in. His eyes narrowed and a red flush crept up his neck. "I don't see how your mom would approve of having an ex-con next door, with her being an invalid and all."

Low blow, insulting asshole. "What Mom approves of is none of your business. Kinda like who Caleb hires."

Clinton shook his head. "It's twice my business since my land borders both of yours. If I catch him trespassing, can I trust you to do your job?"

"While we're on the topic of trespassing, maybe you oughta remember it goes both ways."

Clinton rose to his full height, which was considerably taller than her. She continued to recline against the bar like she didn't have a care in the world.

"What's that supposed to mean?"

Trina plopped the beer bottle on the counter and looked between the two of them.

"If you don't know, then you have nothing to worry about." Farah laid her money on the bar and sauntered away. That little conversation would probably make things worse. She'd have to tell Dad and see if he could fit in an extra sweep of their property each night. Same with Caleb.

Stress wasn't a wall of floodwater that slammed into her, it was a slow trickle that eroded her foundation, threatening to topple her over. She'd gotten to Clinton and he wasn't going to ignore it. She'd also alluded to knowing he was tampering with their property. He'd either get sneakier or more blatant.

"Thanks, man." Caleb grabbed the beer from her. "You wanna go after this or stay for one more?"

She refrained from glancing at Clinton. "I should get home and check the cattle before it gets dark."

He pulled out his phone and thumbed on the screen for her to read.

Checked our herd and the James cows. All good. Jesse.

Max glanced between them. With his shaggy salt-and-pepper hair and stocky build, his ability was often underesti-mated. People, especially those he pulled over, assumed he couldn't pursue them on foot more than a quarter mile. But Farah had seen him run through forty acres of pasture to tag kids fleeing a forbidden bonfire on private property.

Max's gaze rested on Caleb. "I heard we all know your new hired hand. Is he going to be a problem?"

Scotty snorted. "Hasn't he already been a problem?"

Caleb took a long pull from his beer before answering. "No to both questions, but I'm not a fortune-teller."

"Take the plug out of your ear and tell me that again." Max chuckled and looked at her. "Farah didn't take him down last night, so I might actually believe he's not guilty of starting the fire at the Walkers. But come on, how long do you think that'll last?"

Her mind immediately went to exactly how she'd taken Jesse down.

"Jesse's cool." If Farah hadn't known Caleb so long, she wouldn't have been able to tell how much effort he was putting into being nonchalant. "He's seen the light and his sister's the most important thing to him. Seriously, he can fix any engine in front of him."

The corner of Max's mouth curled. "It's not his mechanic skills I'm questioning, it's his talent with a lighter. But the guy's gotta have big balls to take a job with a firefighter."

Farah's irritation surged. Was it because Max wasn't letting up, or because she knew for sure Jesse had big— It didn't matter. She'd bet her meager retirement pension Clinton and his brother were behind the Walker fire.

Max's attention turned to her. "And living next to a deputy. Aren't you afraid he'll get back at you for his time in the jail?"

"No." She wasn't going to make excuses or justify why she didn't think so. Only two people at this table had talked to Jesse recently, and they weren't the ones bad-mouthing him.

"Well, I'd be careful if I were you." Max adopted the fatherly concern look he used around rookies. "You know you can't keep any guns in the house with a felon around."

A beat of confusion pulsed in Caleb's gaze before he nodded in understanding. "A felon can't possess or have access to firearms. Don't worry. My shotgun's locked in the gun safe in the basement."

Dammit, she hadn't even thought of that law. It should've occurred to her before now.

Max harrumphed and turned to her. "Maybe start wearing your sidepiece twenty-four seven. I'd bet your mom would agree."

Frustration with herself and Max using her mom to further his argument flipped her into the anger zone. She wasn't a rookie. She wasn't Max's daughter. They were coworkers. "Mom would leave the decision up to me. After you arrested your neighbor for rupturing his wife's spleen, did you start packing? Or do I have to because I have boobs?" The table fell quiet and she tried to lessen the effect of her outburst. "Should Caleb and I get matching pink pistols?"

Scotty grinned, taking the cue to lighten the mood. "Why not? Caleb's already got the matching fuzzy handcuffs."

Rowdy laughter broke out and the group turned their attention to teasing Caleb. She hadn't meant to throw him into oncoming jokes at his expense, but he didn't discourage the conversation. They'd known each other long enough that he had caught how pissed she was. Max was looking out for her but he hadn't passed the same warning on to Caleb. It was unnecessary anyway and that was where her real ire lay.

Frustration and sympathy mingled inside of her, souring the sweet drink on her taste buds. While the guys had been riding her and Caleb, Jesse had provided much-needed security at both ranches. He'd been excluded from the night and yet had still done his job, but between Clinton and the combined police and fire departments, his welcome in Moore was nonexistent.

She was welcoming Jesse into her life when her friends wanted to run him out of town.

JESSE WAS DOZING in bed when the rumble of Farah's truck woke him. Though his door was closed, he heard the back door creak as Caleb entered the house and went straight to his room. Farah drove away.

Jesse peeked at the time. Ten thirty. He and Caleb had an early morning, but calling it quits this early was full-on adulting. He let his eyelids drift closed again, and his thoughts returned to earlier.

He'd had a decent meal with Josie, but his stomach had been in a knot the whole night. What if one of Brock's cousins made an appearance? They hadn't, but it hadn't helped his acute case of acid reflux.

He'd come home early to take the side-by-side and check cattle and fence before sunset. At this time of year, daylight lasted until ten. Doing his job had made him feel useful and eased the tension coiled in his gut.

His phone buzzed.

Can you come over?

He stared at the message from Farah. The phone vibrated again and he nearly dropped it.

There's a back door to the shop. I live in there. Take the path between the trees but watch your step.

His heart sank only slightly. She was asking him to sneak over without being seen.

But she was asking him to come over.

He swung his legs down and sat up. Dressing took a minute and then he was tiptoeing down the stairs. At the bottom, he shoved his feet into his boots without worrying about the ties. Opening the door slowly kept the hinges from squeaking too loud, but tomorrow he'd hit them with some WD40.

Caleb's yard light was enough to get to the trees, but once he hit the grown-in trail between the properties, he had to rely on moonlight, going slow. The Jameses' streetlamp illuminated their yard more effectively than Caleb's. The shop sat on the end of the drive, the Dodge Ram Farah had driven earlier parked outside.

Jesse studied the house as he walked the perimeter. The place was dark except for a downstairs light emanating from the middle of the floor. A hallway light? He didn't care as long as no one came after him with a shotgun.

He switched his attention to the shop. One large door took up most of the sidewall, with only a smaller window on the other side. A small apartment was built into the shop. That was Farah's place?

Going around the back, he found the door and slipped inside. A small nightlight over the workbench led him straight to the wooden entrance that worked as her front door. He tapped on the surface.

It swung open to Farah wearing a soft pink top that hung loose off her shoulders. Jeans molded to her thighs and draped over bare feet. Her hands were stuffed in her back pockets and she couldn't meet his gaze for long.

He pushed the door closed and took a quick look around. It was larger than an economy apartment and had a kitchenette tucked in a corner. Functionality was the theme, as there were few decorations on the walls and no obvious color scheme besides earth tones. A lone lamp was on in the middle of the sitting area, where there was nothing but a couch and a TV.

She glanced behind her like she was trying to imagine what he was seeing.

"What's wrong?" he asked.

Her fervent gaze met his and she launched into his arms. He caught her and thumped backward against the door. When her lips pressed against his, he wanted to ignore the rest of the world and concentrate on her taste.

Sweet with no hint of alcohol.

He returned the kiss but then set her down and pulled away. Brushing a hand down her cheek, he asked again, "What's wrong?"

She hadn't been drinking, so this wasn't a drunken booty call.

She bit her lip, but her hands didn't leave his shoulders and their bodies stayed pressed together, a fact his manhood confirmed.

"The whole time I was having a shitty confrontation with Clinton, you were looking out for me and my family. And I… missed being with you." Her lower lip was caught in her white teeth.

Her insecurity and sincerity did him in, but he had to know where they stood about tonight. Because he'd come prepared.

"I went to town today. Well, not Moore, but I bought condoms."

Her eyes flared and her breath hitched. He didn't miss the tightening of her hands in his black T-shirt. "My bedroom is upstairs."

Then they'd get there. Eventually.

But she had a different plan. She tugged his hand and led him through the sitting area and up the stairs lining the rear wall. Her bedroom was a loft with nothing more than a queen-sized bed and a dresser. It was still bigger than the room he was staying in.

She backed to the edge of the bed, gripped the hem of her shirt, and lifted it up. He didn't do the same with his own shirt, too paralyzed by the sight of creamy skin bared to her simple cotton bra. The shirt hit the floor.

His lips parted and his mouth watered at the thought of nibbling along her smooth neck down to the pink peaks visible underneath the flimsy material.

When she flicked the fly of her pants open, he jerked. She was serious. This was happening and she didn't want to play sensual games.

He ripped his shirt off and this time she stalled while rolling her pants down.

"Let me," he said gruffly.

Hooking his fingers in the waistband, he dragged her jeans off, kneeling as they went down. He dropped a kiss on her rounded stomach, loving her lush curves. Her waist nipped in but was lined with soft flesh over defined muscle.

She stepped out of her pants while his own strangled his erection. But it'd have to wait.

Next, her underwear came off. Her breaths came in short bursts as he kissed his way down her belly.

"Lie down," he commanded.

She dropped like her legs had given out and what a rush that was. He lifted one over each shoulder and greedily eyed her damp sex. Her fingers clenched the edge of the bed, buried in the plush blanket that he absently noted had a horse pattern.

He ran his finger through her light curls, testing her wetness.

She gasped, her legs tightening around him. "Jesse."

He'd take his time the next round. He claimed her with his mouth. She bucked into him as his lips closed around her clit. Flicking and licking with his tongue, he waited until her undulations became rhythmic before sliding a finger into her tight, hot channel.

The moan he was rewarded with made it hard not to take her fast. But it was out of his control. Her sex clamped around his finger and she came with force, crying out and arching her back.

He drank her in, unable to believe his day had ended so much better than it had begun.

Her legs went lax and he prowled up her body, one hand digging into his pocket. He withdrew the condom packets and tossed all but one on the bed.

"Don't move." He dropped his zipper and freed his erection. Her legs twined around him, and she watched him, her hair spread around her. This morning, she'd looked like an angel had fallen into bed with him. Tonight, she was his most wicked imagining come to life.

He ripped open the wrapper and rolled on the condom, his shaft straining for her.

He should free her breasts and kiss along her neck until she shivered in his arms, but they both needed what was coming next.

Positioning himself, he dipped his hips until they lined up perfectly. Meeting her gaze so full of anticipation, he entered her—slowly.

She drew her knees to the side, giving him more room. Coming up onto her elbows, she watched him take her.

It was torture not to thrust shamelessly until he came. Which would only take a few pumps before he was done.

This was Farah James. Deputy James. And he was inside her.

When he was seated completely in her wet heat, he slumped over her, his knees wedged against the bed.

She kissed his cheek, then nuzzled his ear.

"I want to make this last," he whispered.

"You have more condoms." She rocked against him. His hips jerked and he slid out and thrust back in. The stroke of her velvet heat was paradise.

Her satisfied gasp was enough encouragement. Propping himself on his arms, he set a hard pace. She wrapped her hands around his wrists and held on to him with her legs.

He pumped, gritting his teeth against the looming orgasm. He should make her come again, but she was right. He had more condoms, and once he got this round out of the way, he could lavish attention on the rest of her.

The climax kicked his arms out from under him. He collapsed over her, helpless against his release. Her heels dug into his ass as he finished inside of her, groaning into her neck.

When he went still, she held him.

Damn, he should be embarrassed. He'd come in her hand last night and tonight he'd barely lasted a minute. But she seemed to enjoy her effect on him and fuck, he'd come in two seconds if it stroked her ego.

Because he'd made her orgasm within minutes, too.

Rolling off her, he rose off the bed and shucked his pants. Kicking them next to his shirt, he glanced over his shoulder at her.

"Now we can get started."

CHAPTER 11

Farah rolled her hips, sinking onto Jesse until he was so deep she didn't know where he ended and she began.

A few hours had passed, and they were on their last condom. She believed him when he said it'd been a while for him. Each time he lasted longer, but the effort showed and she loved it.

He'd broken his abstinence for her, almost like he'd waited for her. It should freak her out, but it wasn't like he'd hung up pictures of her in his cell and called to hang up on her.

He acted like she was his dream woman and she liked it.

Rising again, she meant to tease him, but Jesse had a breaking point. He was under her as she rode him, but he rolled up, catching her in his strong embrace.

His lips planted over the pulse at her throat. His arms wound around her until his hands dug into her ass cheeks.

"I was going for sensual," she breathed.

"We did slow and sensual last time." His low growl traveled down her belly straight to her sex.

She might be on top, but he took over, lifting and lowering her with such force her breasts bounced.

He released her neck and caught a nipple in his mouth.

Oh God, that mouth.

There wasn't a place on her body he hadn't tasted. After their first quick round, he'd taken his time. Sensual was right. He'd spent an hour playing with her body like she was an engine he'd been dying for a chance to inspect.

Even sitting like he was, he jerked his hips straight into her. The way he filled her, he hit all the right spots. The first rays of a climax shuddered through her.

His teeth grazed her sensitized nipple and he had to be digging handprints into her ass.

He was dominating her. This was nothing like the exploratory college sex she'd had, or the awkward *I'm dating a cop* sex she'd had early in her career before she gave up trying.

This was raw, unfiltered fucking…but with emotion. That last part threatened to do her in.

She tensed and jerked out of rhythm.

He lifted his head from where she was crushing it like a vise in her arms. "It's just you and me right now. We'll figure out the rest later."

How'd he always seem to know what she was thinking?

He reset her pace and she took over, throwing her head back, demanding her pleasure. Though it wasn't like she had to. He gave her body nothing but ecstasy and what he did to her mind was the most dangerous of all. He treated her like Farah James, a woman *and* a deputy.

She switched her hold to his shoulders and her whole body tightened. "Jesse," she cried out, and she was lost to another peak.

He came with her until they both toppled into a tangle of arms and legs.

When her breathing slowed down, she couldn't quit touching him. Her fingers danced along his chest. Her own chest was covered in love marks and red from his attention, but he'd played nice with her neck and any area visible above her collar.

"It's getting late," she said and looked into the brown eyes she'd started seeing in her dreams.

"Yep. You gonna tell me what the deal was at the bar earlier?"

She sighed and rolled to her back. Her skin pebbled despite the warmth gathered under the roof of her loft. He rested his hand on her stomach, his fingers splayed. It was enough of a cocoon against the rest of the world to make her talk.

"Clinton insulted you and my mom and then I hinted that I knew what he'd been up to. And we hardly talked for more than a minute."

Jesse stayed quiet like he wasn't surprised that was exactly how it had gone.

"What I'm really worried about is that I made things worse for you," she admitted.

He rolled up to an elbow, his brow creased. "Me? Why?"

"Because if he can't target me easily, he'll use you to make himself look like the good guy."

Jesse nodded. "It's what guys like him do. I'll watch out for myself." His eyes pinched and he looked away.

"What?" She turned his face back to hers.

"What are we doing here?"

Getting good and fucked, in more than one way. "I don't want to quit this."

A brow arched and a smile played over his lips. Those lips and what they could do... "Me neither. But we can't exactly come out and say that we're seeing each other."

And they weren't really seeing each other, were they?

They were having sex. There was no dating, no meeting the parents, no public outings. She didn't want him to be her dirty secret.

"If it weren't for the recent fire… I mean, it would've been tricky enough to explain to my boss." Sheriff Allred was by the book. And while she'd perused the employee handbook during her last shift, she couldn't find a hard and fast rule about forbidding relationships with people with records. Didn't mean the sheriff wouldn't add one—after giving her an ultimatum, if he didn't outright fire her. "And really, no one should find out before him, and then there's my coworkers…"

"I know."

She sighed. He always said that, and she appreciated his understanding, but she wanted an easy answer that would help them both. "My job is floating this ranch. I can't lose it. Even if I got fired, it's not like there're any good security positions in Moore with the same benefits I get with the county."

"You don't have to explain. I'm not going to ruin anyone else's life." He dropped a kiss on the tip of her nose and skimmed his hand down to cover her mound. "But I'm going to do this every chance you let me."

"Tomorrow night?" She frowned. "Tonight? What time is it?"

"Too late to get a decent amount of sleep. Sorry."

"No, I'm sorry. My dad always lets me sleep in after my monthly night out. By the time I'm awake to help Mom, he'll take off fishing."

Interest lit his eyes. "Your dad likes to fish?"

"'Like' is an empty word for describing Dad and fishing. He's obsessed."

Jesse's smile was faint, but it reached his eyes. "My dad loved fishing. Did I tell you he drowned fishing?" She nodded. It hurt to hear him say it. "He went out fishing on the boat instead of casting from the shore any time he could. I was too much of a handful for him to take along."

She saw echoes of that wild, sad little boy when he talked about his dad. "Did you ever get to go?"

He shook his head. "Bill wasn't into it, but you can be damn sure Mom put me through swimming lessons."

"Your dad didn't know how to swim?"

"Nope. Even with a life jacket, he didn't make it, but the boat knocked him out when it flipped. So I guess it wasn't exactly about how proficient he was. I still wonder if things would've been different if he'd known how to swim."

And from his tone, he frequently thought about how different.

"Since you get to sleep in"—he relaxed next to her, rolling to his back—"what are you and your mom doing today?"

"I'll run through her therapy with her and see where Dad's at with the ramp we're building into the house. Mom can't do stairs. We thought she'd… She just can't tackle stairs. She can go up easier, but going down, one of us needs to be in front of her, but it's still slow going."

"That's rough."

"Yep." Jesse was the first person she'd talked to about it. Caleb always asked and was willing to lend a hand, but Farah had adopted an optimistic attitude in front of everyone, including her friends. "She's made a lot of progress, but it's clear she'll never get back to where she was. We can help her be stronger and learn to use what control she has. If feels like our goals shift every month."

He asked about her mom's therapy while covering them with her blanket. They talked about her mom, his mom, then what life had been like as a kid for each of them. Subjects like his stepdad and Bill didn't come up.

Eventually, she drifted off and when she woke to the sun

beating down on her bed, Jesse was gone. She didn't know when she'd see him again, but she knew she wanted it to be soon.

~

JESSE WHIPPED the newly repaired four-wheeler to the left along the fence to cut off the cow that thought she could skirt away from the rest and stay in the current pasture.

Once he and Caleb got all the girls and their calves settled in the summer pasture, he stopped his four-wheeler to help shut the wire gate.

"I can see where this would be easier with horses," Jesse said, adjusting his cap to let a waft of wind cool his scalp. June was hot and humid this year and he'd worked up a sweat just starting the engine.

A good stretch of sleep would've helped, but in the two weeks since he'd first snuck over to Farah's, his nights had been full of welcome interruption. When she wasn't working the night shift, they'd meet at her place, or if Caleb was working, she came to the house. Jesse doubted the springs on his old bed were going to last much longer.

It was easy to pretend nothing was going on. The only people he saw were Caleb and Josie, and sometimes Brock, and if he had to run errands for the ranch or stock up on more condoms, he ventured out of town to avoid someone learning his schedule and setting him up.

There'd been no other attempts to frame him or tamper with the ranches. He kept an eye on Farah's land but steered clear of her dad if he was out working. The last thing Jesse needed was Mr. James suspecting him of being the one causing harm to his property. Farah didn't need that conflict in her life.

"Horses would be nice, but the pasture they used to be

kept in needs new fence." Caleb grinned. "Want that to be your July project?"

"I'm gonna invent an indestructible fence and retire rich off ranchers everywhere."

"Not until you help me install mine first."

Jesse chuckled. "I'd give you a deal." He didn't mind fixing fence. It was honest labor that got him outside. The variety of work his job entailed had grown on him. He'd been a mechanic his whole life, long before he'd earned the official degree. It'd been his identity, one he'd given up everything for, only now it wasn't his complete identity.

If Caleb were to toss him out on his ass, Jesse had a skillset to fall back on. He'd gotten his degree, he had years of experience, and there was no reason—but his fear of rejection—he couldn't apply to respectable garages. Work as a hired hand was always an option, and he was starting to like it as much as working on engines.

Each day that he toiled in the sun, drove cattle, and watched over calves and their mamas made prison seem like a bad dream. The longer he put between him and time served, the less he dreamed about waking up in his worn prison jumper and canvas shoes.

His last trip to Alexandria, he'd even bought a baby blanket for his future niece or nephew. He'd been enamored with the soft material, and the little car stitched into the corner had sealed the deal. It was yellow, a cheerful color Jesse wanted the baby to associate with him. He'd be the fun uncle. Not the ex-con uncle no one wanted to talk about.

Caleb hopped back into the ATV he'd borrowed from Farah's dad. "Let's check the bulls while we're out here." He was going to say more, but his phone blared an emergency alarm.

Jesse shook his head and smirked. Caleb claimed his ringtone could wake him from a dead sleep, but Jesse thought he liked the humor of a fireman with an alarm ringtone.

While Caleb talked to whoever had called him, Jesse walked the fence. He couldn't drive away to give Caleb privacy without the engine drowning out the caller's words.

"Jesse, Derrick James had a clutch go out on his tractor. Want to lend a hand?"

Jesse raised his brows as his heart rate increased. Work next to Farah's dad like he was nothing more than Caleb's hired hand? *God no* was his real answer, but that'd look hostile and suspicious. He couldn't avoid the neighbors forever. How bad could it be?

"Sure." He'd never been bothered when meeting his exes' parents. Probably because he hadn't thought long-term with past girlfriends, and others' opinions of him had been a nonissue. He hadn't cared.

But just the thought of meeting Farah's parents was bringing on a sudden onset of nerves. Because he cared what Farah thought of him—and what Derrick and Corinne James thought of him, too.

Caleb's "See you in a few" blew by on the wind. Then Caleb fired up his side-by-side and took off.

Jesse had a million questions. Shouldn't he stop and grab his tools? Was Caleb sure Mr. James didn't mind Jesse helping? Did Caleb know Farah was working? But he followed Caleb through the pastures. They hit the road and took it the rest of the way to the Jameses'.

He hadn't entered Farah's place from this way. The path between the trees was probably getting worn down, but it was usually dark, or really early morning, and Jesse had never stopped to admire the view.

The two-story, aging farmhouse stood proudly. Unlike Caleb's place it'd been well cared for and was probably thirty years newer. The powder-blue paint should look garish with the red barns and the off-white shop, but the white trim and navy shutters tied the package together. The house was cute, like the woman who was never far from Jesse's thoughts.

The rest of the yard was also tidy. Old or infrequently used equipment lined the outside of the shop, but Farah and Mr. James regularly beat back the weeds to keep the look clean. Horses grazed in the small, square pasture behind the barn, their tails swishing the bugs away.

The doors to the shop were open and dammit, couldn't Mr. James have at least pulled the tractor out? It wouldn't have made a bit of sense, but at least Jesse wouldn't have had to work under the same roof that he did naughty things to Farah under.

He pulled to a stop next to Caleb and shadowed his friend in. Mr. James backed away from the tractor. Jesse forgot his nerves as his gaze swept around the shop. All the equipment was ready to go. Mr. James hadn't pulled the engine out yet, but the lift was ready and tools were scattered across the floor and workbench.

The tractor was older than Jesse, but a clutch replacement should be fairly straightforward. Maybe Mr. James was worried about hurting himself and wanted help.

The older man greeted them, smiling at Caleb, his eyes narrowing on Jesse. Could this be more awkward?

Jesse nodded and tried not hide behind Caleb like a pussy.

Caleb didn't bother with introductions. Perhaps he thought Jesse and Derrick had already met. They should've by now, if Jesse hadn't been avoiding him.

Caleb gestured to the tractor and looked at Jesse. "Be our guest."

The other men hung back and let Jesse take the lead with the clutch. The work was a welcome distraction from the current of tension running between him and Mr. James.

The afternoon was blending to evening when shuffling

caught his attention. He looked back, wiping his sweaty face on the sleeve of his shirt, and paused with his wrench midturn.

A stern woman was gazing back at him. She shared the same eye color as Farah, but her hair was a few shades darker than Farah's sun-bleached color. One corner of her mouth dipped in a frown while the other was a tight not-quite smile. She leaned on a four-legged cane, but Jesse would never consider her weak. Despite the way her right arm was held into her side and her shoulder drooped, she radiated strength and determination.

It must've been a severe stroke, or this woman would be out here throwing engines around. And probably him, too.

Caleb ditched the tractor and jogged over to lay a kiss on her cheek. "Corinne. How's it going?"

She dipped her head, her gaze returning to Jesse.

"Ma'am," Jesse said, straightening.

Mr. James wiped his hands and abandoned Jesse at the tractor, too. "We're almost done. Getting hungry?"

"Lemonade." She said the word deliberately, working hard on the *l.*

Caleb smiled and he pumped a fist in the air. "I'll go grab it."

"Glasses and napkins, too," Mr. James called after him. "Oh, and find a snack, please."

Before Jesse could panic, he was alone with Mr. and Mrs. James. He glanced from one to the other as they faced him. Had this been planned?

He rubbed his hands together like he could get the grease off with his imagination. There was probably a rag around, but with two shrewd pairs of eyes focused on him, he couldn't poke around for it like a dumbass.

"Jesse, have you met my wife?" Mr. James asked.

"No, sir, but Caleb has nothing but nice things to say."

Jesse stepped forward to shake hands but looked at his greasy hand and stopped. "Nice to meet you."

Those eyes didn't leave him. Their effect was no different than any other police officer or parole officer he'd interacted with in the last several years.

Mrs. James lifted her chin, but her gaze remained wary.

Her husband faced her, threading the rag through his fingers. "Jesse here is quite the mechanic. This should've taken me all weekend but looks like I'll get to fish tomorrow after all."

Sunday was his fishing day, and Farah had mentioned she was off tomorrow. He'd planned to meet her tomorrow night. She'd said she'd be home too late and needed to be up by the time her dad left. Jesse was intensely glad he had no secret plans to hook up with Farah tonight.

"Do you fish?" Mr. James asked.

"Uh…" Words escaped him. He grimaced at his lack of finesse and forced himself to continue. "My dad was an avid fisherman, but I've never been out myself."

"Your dad never took you?"

"He, uh, died when I was little. My mom didn't fish and my stepdad"—was a piece of shit—"didn't either."

Mrs. James's scrutiny increased until Jesse planted his feet to keep from squirming.

"Was your stepdad the car guy?" Mr. James asked.

"Yes, sir."

"Call me Derrick." He chuckled. "I can't speak for my wife. You can try Corinne, but I'm surprised she doesn't make me keep calling her Sheriff."

Mrs. James broke her standoff to roll her eyes. Jesse chuckled, a welcome release for his anxiety.

Derrick considered him. "Why don't you come with me tomorrow?"

Jesse's mouth opened, but what the hell could he say? Fishing with Farah's dad?

"Caleb gives you a break once in a while, right?"

Speaking of Caleb, where the fuck was he? "Yes, but my days off vary." He couldn't say no, and a strong part of him didn't want to. Fishing was Derrick's off day and he'd invited Jesse along. Maybe it was just for interrogation, but it was a significant invite.

Derrick's marginal smile reached his eyes. "I'd really like a chance to get to know the man my daughter is seeing."

"I-I—" Shit! "She'll get in trouble if anyone finds out." Was that all he could come up with? He'd never been a smooth talker, but what skills he had were failing him at a critical time.

"And…that bothers you?" Mrs. James asked.

"Yes, ma'am. I…care about her. A lot."

"Well, we aren't naïve," Derrick said. "I've seen you both sneaking around, but Farah's an adult and we don't have to agree with her decisions." Clearly, they didn't. "I might as well get to know the guy she's risking her reputation and career for."

Jesse bit down on his tongue against the sudden shot of guilt. He wasn't risking himself, maybe his work, but it was temporary anyway. And his reputation could only go up. Farah was the one risking it all—for him.

A door slammed and they all whipped their heads around to peer out the shop door. Caleb was descending the ramp with a load of food and drink.

"I'm leaving at eleven sharp if you're up to it." Derrick gave him one last intent look before going out to help carry items.

Jesse couldn't stand awkwardly for the twenty seconds it'd take for the others to get back. And Mrs. James was still inspecting him like gum on her shoe, trying to figure out when it had gotten there and how much yuck would remain if she scraped it off.

"I don't want Farah's reputation ruined, Mrs. James." But he wanted Farah for himself. Could he be selfless enough to let her go?

"I believe you think that." Spoken slowly, but with extreme clarity. Corrine James pivoted, needing to do it three times before she was facing the door, and picked her way out of the shop and away from him.

His decision was made. Whether he and Farah worked out or not, whether her coworkers found out and turned on her, he had to go fishing with Mr. James. Jesse had gotten to know himself in the last several years. His real self. Not who Bill said he was, not who his girlfriends thought he was, but who he really was. Jesse Rodriguez.

And the more he worked with cattle, the fewer times he had to count down from ten or bang out burpees. And the more he was coming to the conclusion that he wasn't a bad guy.

He liked Farah. She risked a lot to see him, but he was willing to be patient. The least he could do was win over Derrick and Corinne James so they could know their daughter hadn't lost her head over a bad man. Jesse would do what it took to prove it. He would do his time.

CHAPTER 12

*J*esse finished his morning chores, including mowing the ditches. Later, he'd rake the clippings into rows for haying like Caleb had showed him. But today was about the fishing.

He grabbed the lunch bag he'd packed after Caleb left. Handling any of Caleb's questions would've required more evasiveness than Jesse was ready for. Then again, it was Caleb. He might've just said "cool" and gone on with his day. No one else knew where he was going other than the Jameses, excluding Farah, unless her dad had mentioned something.

Guilt eked into his calm. In hindsight, he should've called and told her. But he hadn't wanted to disturb her at work, then upset her rest. And if he spoke the plans out loud, *he* wouldn't have gotten any rest.

He should've called when her shift was done.

Jesse went out the door and started for his truck. Wait. Farah's parents had said they could see him going back and forth between the trees. He might as well walk there.

Nearing their place, Farah's laughter drifted through the

trees. He emerged from them, grateful for the cooling breeze. His rising body heat had nothing to do with the weather but everything to do with the hammering of his heart.

Farah's back was to him and he stole a moment to drink her in like he'd gone without water all week. She was in one of the tank tops she favored—purple today—and the hip-hugging jeans that draped over her boots. Was she going riding today?

Derrick was in the middle of speaking, but his eyes lit with surprise and he stopped. Farah glanced over her shoulder, her expression frozen.

Yeah. He understood her shock, couldn't believe he was here either. Her gaze swept over his plain red lunch bag and metal water bottle. She looked like she was about to ask what was wrong, but her dad broke in.

"You made it." Derrick smiled at Farah. "I asked him to go fishing today."

"Oh…really?" She sounded like she knew it was more than a friendly gesture.

Jesse reached them and stopped. If he survived this encounter, he might make it through the rest of the trip without throwing up.

Where'd all these emotions come from? His diet of anger and righteousness had given way to…what? Timidity? Crippling insecurity? Raging self-consciousness? No, he wasn't good enough for the man's daughter. But as long as Farah let Jesse next to her, he couldn't keep his distance.

Jesse hadn't been lying yesterday. He cared for her. A lot. And dammit, he worried about her. He was left to deal with these feelings. This wasn't the time to burst into burpees or race across a pasture in a four-wheeler. The stress turned into nausea instead.

He'd gone from a life of not giving a shit to feeling too much.

"Fishing, huh?" she asked lightly, but the serious gleam in his eyes said she knew he faced an entire day of thinking about his father.

"Yeah," Derrick answered. "You two seem to be spending a lot of time together, so I thought I should find out who Jesse Rodriguez is."

Farah's face flushed and Jesse shot her an apologetic smile. Would her parents think less of her?

She lifted a light brow, one hand slamming onto her hip. He wanted to explain his reasoning, but it'd just sound like the excuses they were. He hadn't wanted to hear that she thought it was a horrible idea.

Farah looked between them and settled her gaze on him. "Then I'll pull steaks out and you can come over for supper."

The hard edge to her voice didn't deter his stomach.

"To grill?" Jesse almost moaned his question. They might have an oven, but it'd been too hot to prepare anything more than hamburger hot dish on the stovetop. And he still refused to touch anything that dealt with fire after the scene with Clinton, just in case.

Farah's expression softened and her hand dropped from her hip.

Derrick chuckled. "You sound like a starving man. Go on, get in. We'll be back the normal time."

He got in and Farah walked Jesse around to the passenger side.

"Are you sure you're okay with this?" she asked softly.

No, he was dying inside. "Of course. It's just fishing."

"Alone. In a boat. In the middle of a lake."

He frowned at the two-toned brown boat hooked to the back of the pickup. It wasn't large, but then he knew nothing about boats. "Are you afraid for him or for me?"

She tugged on his arm before he opened the door. "I didn't mean for it to sound like that."

"It's okay. I'd better not keep him waiting."

He got into the passenger seat and gave her a wave without looking at her. Little reminders like that were good. He was ready to do anything to prove himself; he couldn't storm away at the first test. Him being alone with Mr. James made Farah nervous. Her reaction made it clear where he stood with people, including the girl he was seeing.

Too easily, he forgot this flame between him and Farah could get extinguished as thoroughly as the fire he'd started five years ago. He just hoped she wasn't the one stomping on the flames.

∼

FARAH CHECKED the propane and started the grill. The wait was killing her.

Dad was the easygoing one of her parents, but what if he scared Jesse off?

What if he didn't?

The last two weeks had been…hot. Sizzling. Scorching. She'd never had so much sex in her life. She'd never *wanted* to have so much sex. Even worse was how she looked forward to cuddling afterward. They talked.

She'd never talked to her dates. They'd wanted the gossip from her job, to hear badass stories. But Jesse didn't know who ninety-year-old Maggie Morris was or how her yacht of a Cadillac had taken on a buck and won. Or that Mrs. Morris hadn't noticed and had driven home with a fender full of guts, and then her son had called, worried that his mom had hit a jogger.

She'd made the mistake only once during a date of bringing up something from her day. One mention of an elderly woman getting her license yanked and the guy's eyes had lit up. *Was it the Morris lady?* He'd laughed about his friend who worked for the county and had cleaned up the remains of the deer. Farah hadn't found the story as humorous as it was tragic. Mrs. Morris had lost her license and therefore her ability to live alone. That was when Farah had written local men off her list of eligible options, and all men who thought her job was a party.

Jesse only listened as she vented her frustrations about how after five emergency calls for domestic abuse, Brittany Collins hadn't left her abusive husband, instead defending him to the point where she'd gotten arrested—when Brittany had been the one to call 9-1-1 in the first place.

And damn if Farah shouldn't be talking to Jesse like that. Names. Places. Details. But she'd gone to school with Brittany. The girl had married a guy twice their age and was on her third kid. And those kids were either witnessing mommy getting beaten or getting it themselves.

Sure, she and Caleb were close, and when they faced brutal emergencies that left them ragged and torn, they talked about it. But it was usually when they'd gone through it together. If he was called to a rollover for the Jaws of Life and Farah was on the same call to notify loved ones of a death, then they got together for a couple drinks to wallow in their emotions.

But the everyday shit? She had no one.

Mom would listen, but she'd stress and Farah couldn't do that to her.

Wandering back into the house, she was about to check her phone for the eightieth time. Mom was at the counter, shaking salt onto a pile of steaks. The KC seasoning, pepper, and garlic powder bottles lined the dish.

"They're on their way." Mom hadn't said much about Jesse. She probably wanted Dad's take on him because she trusted his somewhat unbiased opinion over Farah's.

Couldn't blame her. Farah couldn't trust herself around

Jesse. He'd bypassed all her good sense as soon as she'd learned he was legitimately helping Caleb out. It was enough redemption for her hormones, and unlike the deputy in her, they didn't care about his past as long as his present was on the right side of the law.

The deputy in her was starting not to care either. But it wouldn't be the same for the other deputies.

"Thanks for seasoning the meat," Farah said. She went to the fridge, opened it, and stared. What had she gone there for? Closing the door as she spun, she went to the cupboard and grabbed four glasses. Oh yeah, lemonade. She set the cups down and went back to the fridge.

Why hadn't she just brought the cups to the table?

She set the jug of lemonade on the counter and turned back to gather the glasses. When she spun around, Mom was staring at her, the KC seasoning bottle in her left hand.

"What?" Farah looked around. Had she dropped something?

"Scatterbrained is not your thing." It took Farah a moment to work out the word Mom called her, her slur making it sound like *shatterbrained*.

Farah glanced around. She wasn't acting differently. Yeah, maybe she'd lost count once or twice during Mom's exercises for therapy. And she'd had to go back to clean the other half of the bathroom after she'd walked out an hour earlier to check her phone and forgotten to go back.

"I'm nervous," Farah admitted.

"You should be." Mom shook powder onto their dinner. "But not about us."

"Of course I'm worried about you. If Jesse doesn't get your stamp of approval, he'll never get—" Farah glanced away. Was she even considering this?

"Coworkers' approval?"

"I don't know how long Jesse's going to be here." The

truth rang between them. She'd concluded he was still in Moore for her and his sister. Since Josie hadn't ditched her brother yet, Jesse could go anywhere with her support.

He hadn't saved up enough money to buy another vehicle, but again, Josie would help him out if it was critical. He could go anywhere, but he was staying close enough to meet Farah each night she was free.

"My guess is…" Mom carefully put the cover to the seasoning back on, twisting it with one hand. She worked hard to enunciate her next words. "He's not leaving. Not until you tell him to."

"Both hands, Mom."

Her scowl was as comical as it was heartbreaking. As Mom focused on her right arm's fine motor skills, she said, "What is… Jesse's future? What's his plan?"

"To be Uncle Jesse."

Mom glanced up from her task. Was she surprised that Farah didn't need to think about it, or that there wasn't much to answer?

"He's saving up for a vehicle of his own without his sister's help. But she's due in four months, so I think he plans to be around. And… I think he likes ranching."

Farah wasn't the only one who talked in bed. Jesse talked about his day like a kid whose toy tractors came to life. He'd been so angry in jail, but now he was excited. Optimistic, even if his future was uncertain. He knew he had one, and where he'd only seen low pay because of his ex-con history and a life full of trying to stay out of jail, now he had options, choices that were his own, not his stepdad's. Not even Josie's. Jesse's confidence that he could lead a normal life that didn't include drifting from shit job to shit job was obvious. Farah was proud of him.

Not proud enough to be seen in public with him. She

frowned. How long would either of them be content to sneak around like they were?

Mom pushed away the bottle, its top successfully screwed in place. "Well. Ranching is in his blood?"

"He's proving he's changed." Farah adjusted her armload of glasses. She didn't sound like those spouses she helped, did she? *He's changed. He's really trying.* Or in the case of Rodney Mills as he was getting a fingernail gash on his face stitched up, *Oh, it's that time of the month. She always gets a little crazy during that week.*

The flat look her mom gave her said she was thinking the same thing. Probably even about Rodney, since his wife had been beating him since after the motorcycle accident twenty years ago that had left her with a traumatic head injury. He made all the excuses in the world for his wife. Mom had heard them all and now it was Farah's turn.

She wasn't an overly optimistic family member with blinders on, claiming her loved one couldn't have possible stolen her account numbers and cleaned out the bank— again. Jesse could've made life hard on Josie, refusing to be around Brock, but he'd accepted the man as family and respected the Walkers' need for distance. He could've lost it on Clinton in the store and he hadn't. He could've walked away from her dad and his invitation, but he was out on a boat, trying to prove he wasn't a loser they should give up on.

"I want tonight to go well and then I'll worry about work." She concentrated on pouring lemonade and setting the table.

Tires crunched on the gravel. Farah nearly sprinted to the door.

Male laughter reached her before she spotted them. The guys were already out of the pickup, unloading tackle boxes and rods.

Dad placed a cooler on the ground. "Hey. Hope you got

plenty of steak out." Dad lifted his cap and readjusted it. "Cuz we ain't gonna contribute a whole lot."

"Nothing biting?" Farah asked, looking at Jesse.

He grinned. "Not by the time we got me set up with a license."

Dad chortled. "We drove all over that damn lake looking for enough signal to get him a fishing license online with our phones. Geez, I think we only got an hour or two in with lines in the water. We were on the damn boat before we even thought of it." Dad grinned, his eyes sparkling. "But we got this boy his first fish."

Farah smiled. She remembered her first fish with Dad: a smallmouth bass that had tipped the scale at all of two pounds. Dad had been so excited, she'd glowed like she bagged Jaws.

Jesse lifted the cooler to head for the house. As he passed her, he shot her a grin. "I heard my first was bigger than yours."

The comment was so unexpected, she gasped. "I'll have you know I was six years old."

"A fish is a fish," he teased.

She was still smiling as she helped Dad put his gear away in the garage.

"He's a good kid." He paused after setting his load down. "He needs an outlet like fishing. When we couldn't get a signal and he worried he'd messed up my fishing day, I could tell he was strung tighter than my line with a record-breaking northern pike on the end. He needs more than work in his life, or just like my fishing line, he's going to snap." Before she could reply to Dad's insight, he patted her on the shoulder. "Come on. Let's get cooking. My sandwich burned off hours ago."

She trailed behind him to the house. If Jesse's afternoon had gone well with Dad, Mom was going to warm even more to him before the end of the night. But Farah's anxiety didn't drain away. *He's going to snap* echoed in her mind. But it brought up her conversation with Mom. What else did Jesse do besides work and spend time with her?

He couldn't avoid stress forever. She wasn't always around, and she couldn't be the anchor for his change. He had to do it by himself, or they couldn't be together.

CHAPTER 13

It'd been a week since Jesse had lived through the most stressful day of his life. How could meeting the Jameses be worse than court?

Because he'd had all his righteousness in court. Farah had been nothing more than a cute jailer and a pipe dream. At the time, she hadn't made him want to be a better person.

But now he did. He wanted to contribute to society, to his family, to his own future. And he wanted to keep seeing Farah.

Speaking of. Jesse glanced at his phone for the hundredth time and tucked it back into his pocket. He was in Caleb's kitchen. The guy was on duty and Jesse had prepped the ditches to hay after the grasses dried. He liked haying, just like he enjoyed mowing, with or without the riding lawn mower. It was meditative and required enough physical exertion to relax him.

He shouldn't have anything to stress over. The necessities were provided for. He had enough money to buy food, send Dillon a check, and sock away for a vehicle and place of his own. Caleb was giving him all the time he needed to get back on his feet.

Farah's parents accepted him. Derrick James even *liked* him. Corinne might not be as warm and fuzzy, but he'd actually made her laugh when he and Derrick had regaled her with their fish-license drama.

So what was eating at him?

Jesse rolled his neck. Times like this, he regretted not seeing a shrink. He couldn't be doing burpees or mowing all the time, but his emotions didn't care. What happened if he couldn't identify what was bothering him? Or when he couldn't do anything about it?

Like how he and Farah had been sleeping together for weeks and hanging out with her parents for the last week, but they were still a secret from the rest of the world. He'd asked her about telling Caleb and Josie, but the flat line of her mouth had been eloquent. She'd asked to wait until she spoke to her boss.

He wanted to be with her. She was worth the wait. So he'd have to wait.

But when he'd finally reached the point of not being ashamed of himself twenty-four/seven, he'd also had another realization. He didn't want to be her dirty little secret.

Adjusting his shoulders to relieve the tension radiating through them, he focused on his task. His work was nearly done. All he had to do was roll his preparations. Spread in front of him on the counter were wraps, garden-veggie cream cheese, lunchmeat, and chopped olives. He was packing a damn picnic, his first ever. His mom used to bring these pinwheel things to every potluck she'd dragged him to, and each time he'd devoured half the batch before they'd left the house. He was confident he could recreate them based on taste.

And maybe a quick text or two to Josie.

He was meeting Farah when she got off work at five. These would keep if she worked later and he could always find a project to tinker with. He'd already lubed the door hinges so as not to wake Caleb up sneaking to Farah's place. But the sink in the first-level bathroom was leaking, the corner of the dining room flooring had worked itself loose, and it'd take minutes to slap a fresh coat of paint in his own room. He had it all taped off and ready to go.

The heat and humidity were sweltering this year and he and Caleb had taken to indoor projects in the afternoon.

His phone pinged. *I'm done. Want to ride out for the picnic?*

He hadn't ridden a horse since that first time, but since Caleb was searching auctions and gathering prices, Jesse had better learn while he could.

Sure. Be right over. Deftly rolling each wrap, he loaded them into the cooler as he finished. They rested on top of the cold and perspiring cans of sparkling strawberry water and baggies of grapes.

Fuck, sometimes he didn't recognize himself.

And that was a good thing.

He zipped the cooler shut and left the house. They'd planned to hang out at the copse of trees separating the far end of her land and Caleb's. It bordered Clinton's land, but his piece was an entire section and the farthest point from his house.

He and Caleb had found several areas of weak fence in the past week but couldn't identify it as anything more than a hungry cow pushing on the wire to get to the lush grass on the other side. The cattle they'd moved earlier were doing okay, but Jesse was checking them more frequently. He couldn't pinpoint what was wrong other than they were more vocal than usual, but his gut said something was off and he'd shot a message to Caleb. They'd take a closer look in the morning.

As he crossed through the trees, he noted his trail was getting well worn. The yard and house were quiet. The Jameses must've retreated inside for the afternoon and evening. Farah had mentioned the extreme temps were harder on her mom.

The horses nickered by the barn. Farah must be there getting them ready. He went straight through the open doors, picked his way through the packed straw, and went out the other side.

Petunia and Lily Fields were already saddled. Farah's hair was down. The ridge from her bun was combed out but still visible. She was in regular clothes, including jeans with bedazzled back pockets to show off her rounded ass and his favorite, her tank top. This one was light blue, a nice contrast against her bronzed skin. Watching the flex of her muscles was one of his favorite pastimes.

At the shuffle of his boots on the floor, Farah glanced up, both lead ropes in her hand. "Hey." Her smile was all Farah. He hadn't seen her as Deputy James since the night he was framed. She handed Petunia's rope over.

"We're getting right to it." He hooked the cooler's shoulder strap across his back and swung up. He could breathe again. His first time getting on a horse had gone well, but he hadn't wanted to ass-plant, assuming he could do it again.

Farah followed suit. "As long as you're okay with it."

He snorted. "As long as Petunia knows what to do."

Farah grinned, and like a lovesick teenager, his heart flipped. She was gorgeous. Sexy. And though she'd kill him if he said it, adorable.

Farah clicked her tongue and Lily Fields moseyed out of the barn. He barely had to do anything with Petunia. Technically, he was learning nothing more than being comfortable on a beast that could pound him into the ground. Working on cars came with its own dangers, but the vehicles didn't have a mind of their own. The newer ones, with the onboard GPS, rear cameras, and crash sensors, lost their intelligence when they were turned off. Unhook a few wires and boom. Dumb car.

Not so with a horse. He was the novice and Petunia treated him like one by doing all the work. She followed Farah and he stayed in the saddle.

The view was even better than when he was out on the four-wheeler. When he was working, he drove fast enough to require his attention on the path and not the scenery. Yet now that he had all the time in the world to sightsee, he barely cast a glance toward the green fields or the scant, wispy clouds in the expansive blue sky. His gaze was glued to the sway of Farah's hips. Her shoulders were square, her chin up, but she rode relaxed, her thighs hugging the saddle and her body rocking with the gait of the horse. They rode as one. If Petunia picked up the pace, he'd resemble a sack of Yukon Golds and give Petunia a backache.

After twenty minutes, the trees around their destination appeared. Farah angled them around until they were in the shaded patch, which was on her land. She stopped by a fence post and got down. He did the same, not needing to command Petunia to do a thing. The horse was more interested in the untouched grass by the trees. He tied her off just like Farah did with Lily Fields's lead.

"I brought a blanket to sit on." Farah grabbed a bulky bundle from the back of her saddle. It was a patchwork quilt, much like the one he slept on. As if reading his mind, Farah said, "Caleb's grandma made this for me when I was eight. I've used it for everything and I can still throw it in the washer and dryer."

He helped her spread it out, his mind calculating that there was enough space to stretch out full-length. The thought brought images to mind of them naked and twined together. He kneeled on the corner, a raging erection threatening to make his jeans unbearable.

Farah plopped down in the middle, her feet in front of her, but when their gazes met, her expression went from relaxed pleasure to inferno.

Her pink lips parted. "Have I ever told you that I love it when you wear a plain white tee?"

"This old thing?" he joked. In his line of work, they never stayed white for long. When he got a new one, he wore it a time or two before it was relegated to undershirt or work shirt. In this heat, it'd been more about absorbing as little of the sun's rays as possible.

Her gaze swept over him like a brush fire. What had he said about the pinwheels? They could wait.

He popped the button of his jeans. Farah's tongue darted out to wet her bottom lip. "I thought we were going to eat."

"Oh, we are." He let her read into his words as he bent to tug off one of her boots. Then the second came off. He tossed his cap next to them.

Farah glanced around, but they were in the middle of nowhere and only birds and the swish of the horses' tails could be heard. She undid the clasp to her jeans and rolled them off. Her underwear went with it.

His breath whooshed out. This wasn't a darkened room. At this time of year, it was full sunlight in the evening.

Her legs eased apart and he got down, holding eye contact the entire time. "You think if I make you scream, anyone will hear you?"

Her eyes flared. When she came to his room and Caleb was working, they could be noisy. And she was. He liked the sounds he could wring from her. He wanted to hear them in the great outdoors.

Wedging his shoulders between her thighs, he enjoyed

this picture of her spread before him. Breasts straining against her top. Hair hanging free, strands plastered to her face, the breeze ruffling the rest. And her bare sex open to him. If they never got to be together again, this sight would get him through a lot of long, lonely nights—or make them pure torture.

Lowering his head, he kissed her clit. She arched her back, her fingers digging into the quilt. She was ready for him. A heady thought for a guy who'd been the one staring at her for the last twenty minutes.

Sinking down, he was single-minded about her pleasure. She rocked her hips and groaned when she wanted more. When her hands twisted in his short hair, she was almost there. And when he pushed one finger inside, she was propelled over the cliff. Her sex clamped down on him as she cried his name through her release.

He'd arrogantly thought he'd dodged all the vices. He never drank too much, he wasn't interested in drugs, and he liked food but not to extremes. But Farah was an addiction. Her scent, her taste, her sounds, he couldn't bring her to orgasm enough to ever satisfy himself. Part of the reason was because it was only like this with her. It wasn't about him. She didn't give herself lightly. She was cautious. But they were out here, half naked, and he was about to explode.

Digging the condom out, he pushed his pants down far enough to roll it on. Farah had recovered and rolled up to a seat, only to tug him down on top. He went willingly, guiding his shaft to her center and sinking into her heat.

A moan escaped him. Her legs twined around him as they rocked together. He found her mouth, giving her long, languid kisses that matched his easy pace.

Sliding in and out, he took the pleasure she gave him. And it wasn't just sexual ecstasy, though that was off the charts. She made him comfortable. He sank into her knowing she could take his weight. He could nip and nibble at her lips, along her neck, on her earlobe, and it was like a direct line to where they were connected. He could go fast or slow, hard or barely move, and she wanted it all.

He surged up, his thrusts increasing in force and speed. She arched again, flowing with him, her own need increasing. He carried her to the brink with him and when the pressure built and he couldn't fend off his climax any longer, he rested his thumb on her sensitized clit.

Her hands gripped his shoulders, her eyes losing focus. "Oh, Jesse." When she said that, it was almost like a curse, like she couldn't believe he could strum her body like he did.

He knew exactly when she hit her peak and he relinquished his hold, throwing his head back for a few moments, releasing inside of her, before collapsing onto her.

Maybe it was their location, out in the open, but he felt more exposed than he'd ever been. Emotionally raw. He wanted this woman. He couldn't seem to be himself with anyone other than her. And he wanted everyone to know that she was the one for him.

When their breathing slowed down, she turned her face into his. "What is it?"

Kissing her cheek, he pushed off. They'd talked about this, but he had to let her know how serious he was. And he had to find out if she thought he was worth enough, if they were worth enough, to risk her reputation for.

He turned away to take care of the condom, grateful he'd packed an old grocery bag for garbage. Farah got her clothes back on and by the time he turned around, she was sitting cross-legged, waiting for him.

"I'd like to take you out sometime," he admitted.

"Oh." Her gaze dropped to the expanse of blanket between them. "I'd like that, too."

That was it. Did she mean, she'd like it and too bad it

couldn't happen, or yeah, they'd make a date and shock the town?

"I guess I was wondering..." She licked her bottom lip and he was enraptured by the move. "What are your plans for the future? Are you planning on staying in Moore? How long are you going to work for Caleb?"

Her questions relieved him as much as they troubled him. It wasn't just him and his past that were making her hesitant to move beyond sex. She had no idea if he was dependable or not. If she'd risk her career only to find him packed and gone the next day.

"I don't know." He dug through the cooler and sorted the food. "Josie's due in October, so as long as Caleb needs me, it seems like a good way to be around when she gives birth. Without having to worry about monthly bills, I've been able to sock money away. But it'd still just be a junker to fix up, and I could rent only a small apartment."

Soon, he'd have to worry about becoming a regular member of society with all the woes of health insurance, utility bills, and a stable mailing address that wasn't split between Josie's place and Caleb's, depending on what Jesse needed it for.

Attaining that level of responsibility worried him. Living only to wake up in the morning and enjoy the weather, wear himself out with hard work, and sate himself in Farah gave him a relatively stress-free lifestyle. Add in responsibilities, would the anger and bitterness well back up?

"I'll talk to the sheriff this week."

Jesse bit into a grape and stopped. "Really?"

Her smile was shy and she peeled back the wrap to inspect the insides of the pinwheel. Well, he hadn't cut them, so they were just wraps. "I kinda like you. A lot. And... I think I should be able to decide for myself who I want to see."

Her admission staggered him. Jobs for her weren't plentiful in Moore. He couldn't fool himself about what she was risking, but he couldn't bring himself to tell her not to do it.

RECLINING AGAINST JESSE, Farah finished off her wrap. "You're a good cook."

He chuckled. "I haven't done anything with the new oven but reheat stuff. Wait, one day I made mac and cheese."

"Don't doubt a good mac and cheese." She dropped her empty baggie into the cooler. "Mom still tells me what a nice guy you seem to be. I have to be honest, I didn't think you'd win her over."

"Me either." Jesse peered at her from under his cap brim. "She really liked me?"

"I think so. Her bullshit meter is strong. The stroke didn't ruin it. She'd been in law enforcement since she was twenty-two, so she knows when someone is blowing smoke."

"I bet she's seen it all, even in a small town." He wrapped an arm around her and nuzzled her neck, his lips cool from his drink. "Just like you're seeing it all."

"Just wait until I tell you about the teenagers that I busted last night. They—"

Jesse's head jerked up and he peered off toward Caleb's property.

"What is it?" she asked, looking over her shoulder to see what he might've seen.

"I thought I saw..." He pulled away and rose. "Motherfucker."

He took off at a sprint.

"Jesse!" Dammit, her boots weren't on. She wrestled her feet into them and rolled up. Jesse had leaped the fence and was tearing through the pasture. Farah rushed to the barbed wire and jumped it just like Jesse had. Looking beyond Jesse, she spotted a figure darting through the adjacent fence into Clinton's field.

Jesse didn't let up his pace and he was fast. Farah could only see the back of the guy, but from his shape and hair color, it was Clinton's younger brother, Daniel. And he wasn't faster than Jesse.

"Jesse!" What the hell was he going to do? And why was he chasing Daniel? Sure, the guy had been on Caleb's land, but didn't Jesse realize anything he did to Daniel would only reflect badly on himself?

Jesse was only feet behind Daniel. He put on another burst of speed, losing his hat in the process, and tackled the other man to the ground. Grunts and shouts reached her and within seconds she was at the scene.

"Motherfucker, where is it?" Jesse growled. He'd managed to pin Daniel on the ground and startle him. Why was Jesse searching the man's pockets?

Daniel's fists beat at Jesse's sides, but Jesse batted away more attempts than Daniel could land. A trickle of blood escaped Daniel's nose and his face was beet red. But not Jesse's. His expression was all dangerous determination.

"Where is it?" Jesse said again.

Farah had nothing on her to stop them. This was supposed to be a pleasure ride for a picnic supper. Morphing into a deputy mid-dinner hadn't occurred to her.

"Jesse, enough." She shoved at his shoulder. His glare switched to her, then softened. Anger boiled in his eyes, but he wasn't lost to rage. "Get off him." Jesse blinked. "Now," she said between clenched teeth. Looking between him and Daniel, she filled her voice with authority. "You two will not touch each other. Stand up and stand no less than ten feet apart."

Jesse rocked up, his finger pointing at Daniel. "He was taking pictures."

Her stomach plummeted. Pictures? How much had Daniel seen?

She studied the man standing up across from Jesse. He had dusted himself off and was wiping his nose on his shirt. The tip of his phone was peeking out of his front jeans pocket, but no other photo equipment was on him. "Daniel?"

"He fucking attacked me." Daniel sniffed. "Call the police."

"I am the police." Daniel was younger than her, but they'd grown up together. He knew who she was.

Daniel coughed. "No. You're his girlfriend. I don't trust you. You know what, I'll call 9-1-1."

"Daniel—" She looked at Jesse. Her mind was screaming *no!* Keep everyone else out of this. Keep it quiet. Keep everyone from finding out.

Jesse's jaw flexed. "I don't trust him. He's going to erase those photos. Get his phone."

"I can't just take his phone," Farah snapped.

Jesse jutted his chin up at Daniel. "Show her."

Daniel sneered and it did nothing but make him look like Clinton. "Fuck you." He punched in three numbers and made the call. He took a big inhale and wheezed. Another cough.

Farah bit her tongue. She wanted to lunge for the phone, to search every photo and find out what Daniel knew, but he'd obviously seen enough.

Daniel spoke to the dispatcher while digging in his pocket. Farah was prepared to jump him if he brought out a knife. But it was an inhaler. He sucked on it and stuffed it back into his pocket as a voice resonated out of the phone.

Who'd he get? Melanie? Sean? Delaney? "Yeah, I'm on the north section of my land. I was attacked by that Mexican that works for Caleb Cruise. What? Yeah, he's still here." Daniel's gaze darted between them. "Yeah, I fear for my safety."

Jesse shook his head and stalked away several feet like he didn't trust the ten-foot gap between him and Daniel. She couldn't blame him. She wanted to forget she wore a badge and practice every restraining move she'd ever learned on Daniel's arrogant ass. She'd start by twisting his arm behind his back until he crashed to his knees.

Daniel clicked his phone off, but it took a few seconds longer than it should've.

"What are you doing out here, Daniel?" She fought to keep her voice steady.

He shook his head. "Nope. I'm not talking to you. I'll wait until a real cop gets here."

Jesse spun around, but he didn't advance. "What were you going to do with those pictures? Jack off to them or try to get her in trouble?"

A red flush bloomed up Daniel's already mottled complexion. "I'm not a pervert. The sheriff deserves to know when his employees are dating criminals."

Farah wanted to close her eyes and tip her head back, shout at the heavens. Why now? Why before she could talk to Sheriff Allred herself? She mentally sifted through the schedule. Who was on duty?

Max. Of course. Because why wouldn't he be?

Brody Yates or Cote Yellowbird wouldn't have been any better, but Max was the deputy who'd worked Jesse's case the first time. Not to mention the warnings he'd spewed at the bar. With a long and respectable career with the county, he was the least likely to look favorably on her dating Jesse.

She turned her attention on Daniel. "You came out here to spy on me?" On us?

"I'm not talking to you."

She gritted her teeth. She was still a fucking deputy and she'd done nothing wrong but meet her man for a picnic. But she had to play this straight, couldn't make it look like she was hiding anything. Max needed to come in here, do his job, do what she could be doing right now. And then she'd have to see how much shit she was in.

Jesse trembled. The restraint it took not to beat that smug, insulting look off Daniel's face was hard to control. He had to be related to Clinton, cut from the same dirty cloth. Jesse had greasy rags cleaner than this asshole.

Real cop. Daniel was gunning for Farah, and attacking her credibility through Jesse was the easiest target.

What had the asshole seen? Had he snapped a shot of Farah with her pants down? The thought that their intimate moment had been intruded upon... He squeezed his hands into fists and took another step away from Daniel.

Ten, nine, eight, seven— He couldn't repeat his mantra. He wasn't calm and collected, but he was in control, and that was enough.

Pounding that man's face in would feel too good. Daniel was threatening Farah, making derogatory comments and inferences about her. But acting on his impulse would only prove the bastard right. If he had any hope of helping Farah get out of this with her badge intact, he'd have to be a motherfucking angel.

Dragging in a deep breath, he finished counting down to one as he was exhaling. Just like Luis had taught him to. *Breathe through it, son. Sometimes, breathing is the only thing between us and self-destruction.*

An engine sounded in the distance. All three of them twisted their heads toward the sound.

The deputy driving toward them was using the same path the black pickup had barreled out of. What kind of truck did Daniel drive?

Jesse would bring it up, but Daniel and Clinton were probably shiftier than any prisoner Jesse had crossed paths with.

The deputy was Max. Jesse hadn't dealt with him personally, but between Farah's stories and talking with Josie, he felt like he knew the guy. He was starting this encounter at a serious disadvantage. A city cop named Scotty had officially arrested him, but Max had worked with the Walkers on the vandalism.

Farah crossed her arms, but she didn't walk to greet Max.

The older man got out and sauntered over to them. His squinty gaze landed on Jesse, moved to Daniel, and softened when he looked at Farah. A bushy brow rose. He was dressed in the same uniform Farah wore, but the equipment and gear weren't as bulky and cumbersome on him. Did they not make it to fit a woman, or did the county just not care and order what they wanted?

"What's going on here?" Deputy Max asked, nonplussed.

Daniel shoved a beefy finger toward Jesse. "He assaulted me."

"He was spying on us," Jesse said evenly. He planted his hands on his hips to keep from fidgeting under the hard stare of the deputy.

"Why would he be spying on you?" Max asked.

"Did you know they were dating?" Daniel gestured between him and Farah.

Jesse's respect for Max grew. Shock passed through his face before he schooled his expression back to stern.

"Isn't that against the rules or something?" Daniel asked. "Anyway, I wasn't fucking taking pictures. I was checking my own fence on my own land when he attacked me."

"You were on Caleb's land," Jesse and Farah said simultaneously.

Deputy Max shook his head and addressed Jesse. "Did you attack him?"

This was getting turned on him? He glanced at Farah, but her tight features didn't help his anxiety. "He was trespassing and taking photos of us."

"And he's no longer on your land," Max said as if the answer were plain. "But he's bleeding and accusing you of assaulting him. That's why I'm here."

"But he took photos of us." The rest of Jesse's argument died.

Max raised a brow at Farah. Her shoulders drooped and she looked away. She had the most defeated expression Jesse had ever seen. And until they'd started sleeping together, he wouldn't have classified her as a happy person. She was always serious and that's what everyone except her parents and Caleb saw. Serious Deputy James.

Max sighed. "It's not a crime to take pictures, especially when his land is probably in all the photos. But you attacked him."

"He was trespassing." Why was he talking a damn circle around this? He'd done nothing wrong. Why wasn't Farah saying anything?

Daniel piped up. "He gave me an asthma attack and might've broken my nose."

Jesse glared at him. "I didn't hit you." Daniel's nose had probably hit the dirt when he'd gone down.

"Farah, did this man attack Daniel?" Max asked.

Anxiety flitted through Farah's expression. She rattled off exactly what had happened, and all of it made him look guilty as fuck.

He couldn't look at her.

Max gave a curt nod, like he'd come to a foregone conclusion. "Jesse, I'm gonna have to take you in."

"Max..." Farah stepped closer to Jesse.

"Farah." Max's tone cut off all further conversation. "It'll be easier if you let me do my job and stay out of it."

Blood pounded between Jesse's ears. If only he could go back in time, keep from reacting when he'd seen Daniel sneaking through the tall grasses to get closer to them. But what good would it have done? He'd tried being good, schooling his overreaction—if it could even be considered that—but in the end, his destiny was to take the blame.

He looked from smug Daniel to Farah. She had the grace to appear shocked and dismayed but didn't interfere any further. After all, she'd done enough. He was going back to jail.

CHAPTER 14

Farah breezed into work, trying to look better than her knotted stomach felt. None of the three admin assistants glanced up from behind their shatterproof glass to meet her eye. The meeting with her boss was today. He hadn't read her the riot act over the phone but sent a calm text to meet him today.

Brody Yates was standing by the copier, punching buttons and scowling. He was notorious for getting behind on his reports and being relegated to the office until he got them done before his next shift. It was one of the few times his looks didn't get him out of extra work. He wasn't classically handsome, but his lopsided smile and lanky frame reminded everyone of the mischievous farm kid they'd all had in their life at one point.

When he saw her, his eyes gleamed. "Here for your meeting? He's waiting for you." Before she could stop him, Brody fell in step next to her. "Did you have to post bail for your man?"

Jesse was out on bail? Why hadn't he called? She'd been chewing her nails, waiting to hear from him. "Shut up, Yates."

She didn't normally snap like that, but the mess from yesterday had kept her awake all night. Should she try to see Jesse? Was he going back to jail?

Brody grinned like he hadn't overstepped. "Did he think dating you would give him a get-out-of-jail-free card?"

She glared at him, wishing she could cuff him to his desk. Brody wasn't much older than her, and he was a prick. His reaction was exactly what Farah had anticipated. They'd think she'd been duped by a good-looking guy with a record. Because who else would like little ol' lonely her?

"Don't get pissy with me because you're on report-bitch duty," she hissed and pushed past Brody to enter Sheriff Allred's office. Slamming the door shut behind her, she composed herself. A challenging task under the sheriff's steady stare.

"Deputy James. Have a seat." Matthew Allred was a big, intimidating man. His ink-black hair was cropped short, and his deep-brown eyes bored into a person until they spilled their darkest secrets. He was soft spoken, with a low, gruff voice and the cadence of the Native Americans she knew, but then she'd heard he'd grown up on the Spirit Lake Reservation before his family moved to Moore.

He'd only been sheriff for two years, and she'd only known him to be a fair, albeit politically minded man, but this was new territory. She was the only female deputy and her boyfriend, who had a record, had been arrested.

She perched on the edge of a padded wood frame chair. It was uncomfortable on a good day. Today, every point and ridge dug into her.

"I read the report and I have a few questions," he said in his typical mellow tone.

His pause made her feel like she had to say something. "Okay."

His dark gaze flicked up. He settled back and interlaced

his hands across his abdomen. "Did you know Jesse Rodriguez from his time in our jail?"

She knew what he was getting at, but she only replied, "Yes."

He watched her for a moment, but she refused to ramble like she was a guilt-ridden little girl who'd taken her daddy's car for a joyride.

"You're dating." No accusatory inflection. He said it like he was relaying evidence in court.

Honestly, she had no idea anymore. The sense of betrayal emanating off Jesse when Max had arrested him had choked her. She could make a list of shitty people and put herself at the top. But Sheriff Allred wasn't looking for an explanation of her current status. "Yes."

"For how long?"

"Since after he started working for Caleb Cruise." It was all she could do not to prattle about how well Jesse had been doing, what a good guy he was, how he helped her family, too. The sheriff didn't want to hear any of that.

"So you were most certainly aware of his record?"

"Yes, I was aware of his past." She stressed *past*, but Sheriff Allred didn't react.

"You realize how this looks for you, and for the department."

"I'm aware." Painfully.

"Were you aware that we're one of the few departments without a specific policy against personal relationships of this sort?" He glanced at the sheet in front of him and muttered, "We're sadly out of date that way."

She nodded, swallowing hard.

He slumped with a sigh. "You're a good fucking deputy, James." This didn't seem to be the moment to give her thanks. "I'd hate to lose you. I'd ask why you didn't tell me, but…" He flicked the sheet of paper like he was irritated at every word written on it. "If Rodriguez had had a better lawyer, he'd have only been charged with a misdemeanor."

Jesse had admitted that it wasn't just his lawyer, but his own pride.

"No issues in jail, good conduct in the pen, no problems on probation." Sheriff Allred rubbed the bridge of his nose. "I need some time to process this. Be on notice. There will be no retaliation toward the Bradford brothers from you, no tampering with Mr. Rodriguez's paperwork—not that I'd expect that from you, but I didn't see this coming." The sheriff's expression wavered to reveal deep disappointment, but a second later, he was back to stern. "Stay as far away from this case as possible, and everything you do in the field had better be by the book. By. The. Book. You already have to work twice as hard as your male counterparts to get taken seriously, but now it'll take working five, even ten times harder."

Anger swelled, her throat tightened. *You've worked so hard, now work even harder.* She wanted to say so many things, but she kept quiet. Like he said, she'd have to work even harder to get taken seriously despite her strong work ethic and flawless history.

"Thank you, sir." She got up and walked out.

In the main office, the three admin assistants ducked their heads as she walked past. She didn't notice Brody had followed her out until he shaded her from the sun.

"That bad?" he asked.

"I still have my job, so no," she grumbled. The meeting didn't sit right with her. Sheriff Allred hadn't raged, hadn't insulted her, hadn't fired her. It didn't feel like it, but he was standing by her even though lawyers could use her tarnished image to cast doubt on their clients if she'd had a hand in their case. They'd have to dig hard. Her work was impeccable.

The sheriff might be standing by her to present a united

front and confidence in his deputy to spite the lawyers who tried. But she was as good as on probation. The threat of termination if she messed up was unspoken but clear.

Brody scratched the back of his neck. "How'd it— I mean, why— I just didn't expect that of you."

"Do I question all your dates?" she snapped.

"In your defense, that'd be a lot of questions." Brody's lopsided grin softened her. He was always obnoxious, but he offset it with a healthy amount of self-deprecation.

"I don't bring my personal life to work, and you can imagine why I didn't talk about seeing Jesse."

"I mean, none of us really do. Did you know, I took this one lady home, only to wake up to her laying out all her unpaid traffic tickets and asking me what I could do to help her with them?"

She could so see that happening to Brody. "What'd you do?"

"I said sure, I'll help. I asked her to grab her purse and showed her the return address to send the payments to."

A laugh sputtered from her, the last thing she'd expected to do today. "What's your point, Brody?"

"I don't know. Just that we're human, too. And we're held at a higher standard in some areas, whether we like it or not, whether it's fair or not."

She still wasn't clear on his meaning. "What are you saying, Brody?"

"Just that your standards already seemed awfully high. Maybe you need to make sure Jesse really meets them, or that everyone knows he does."

The door behind them opened and one of the assistants poked her head out. "Deputy Yates, are you done with the copier?"

"I wish. Talk to you later, Farah." He rushed inside.

Farah walked to her pickup with Brody's words in mind.

She had thought Jesse surpassed the expectations of others, but then he'd charged Daniel. And the truth was, Jesse couldn't win. One angry word, one more outburst, it'd only dig deeper the hole he'd started all those years ago. People in Moore were astonishingly forgiving but hugely stubborn. Jesse was an outsider who had hurt one of their own. Add in the tattoos and the grungy look from his work, and all they saw was an ex-con. And she didn't know if he could move beyond that if he stayed in Moore.

~

CAN YOU TALK?

Jesse read the message from Farah. He'd just gotten back to the house and hadn't looked at his phone all morning.

Could he talk? That was about all he could do. Caleb was working and Jesse had spent each minute since he was free hauling water tanks and water for the cattle. Because he'd gotten his ass thrown in jail, he hadn't been around to check on cattle. Caleb had gone out as soon as his shift was over.

Jesse's intuition had been spot on. The cattle were acting off because they hadn't been drinking. And they hadn't been drinking because a dead calf had ended up in the spring-fed pond. Whether the calf had died of natural causes or been put there, they didn't know, and the cows hadn't cared. They weren't drinking the water. Two cows had died and Caleb was nursing three calves back to health.

The cattle were watered and getting better. The pond was cleared of the rotting carcass, but Jesse couldn't say things were back to normal. Caleb hadn't fired him—he was blown away that he hadn't noticed Farah and Jesse messing around —but now Caleb knew how serious Jesse's situation was.

Jesse's arraignment was later this week. Guilty or not guilty. That was the question in the court's eyes. Josie had bailed him out and he'd paid her back, but now his bank account was drained like the first load of water to the thirsty herd.

Why did he stay and tolerate this?

For Farah? He hadn't heard from her until now. It wasn't like he had called his deputy girlfriend to bail him out of jail. She couldn't go to court with him. Well, she shouldn't.

He wanted her there. To have some support. To have someone who didn't look at him like he was Moore's most wanted.

He sighed. *Yeah, where are you?*

Home.

He glanced at himself. His clothing had dried from hauling water this morning, but he was dusty and dirty and there was still a lot of work to do. A lot of work he wanted to do to keep court off his mind.

What if they found him guilty, looked at his record, and threw his ass back in prison? Right now, a thousand-dollar fine and community service would be welcome. He couldn't think about getting found not guilty. The Bradford brothers weren't the darlings of Moore, but they were locals. Jesse didn't stand a chance.

And it pissed him off. Daniel had been trespassing and taking photos of them. Jesse had been an ideal fucking citizen since he'd done his time. He'd been released early because of his good behavior, and while some argued that his sentence hadn't been long enough, he'd done his time, probation and all.

Fine. He wouldn't change clothes. Farah had seen him in a pristine orange jumper and in his opinion, that was much worse than the dusty work clothes he wore now.

He jogged over to her shop and walked in. Tapping lightly on her door and walking in, he looked around.

Her place was quiet. The AC unit was pumping away,

keeping the stifling heat of the rest of the shop at bay. Farah was on the couch. She sat up when he walked through the door. He waved at her to stay seated and took the chair next to her. Cuddling was the last thing on his mind, and it was probably the same for her.

"Hey," she said. "How'd it go?"

"Things haven't changed in the Moore jail in the last five years."

She nodded, and he looked away.

"I have court on Thursday. The judge will decide if there's a case, I guess." During his experience with the legal system, he'd learned that he'd never understand it.

"I think there's a good chance— I mean, I was there and I have a good reputation in court."

"Are you going to go?"

She opened her mouth to speak and stopped. And from the regret in her eyes, he could guess what her answer was. And she must've realized how callous it sounded.

"You're not going." He sat forward on the chair and let his elbows rest on his knees as he stared at the floor.

"I..."

"Because of your job, right?"

"I was called into Sheriff Allred's office. He basically said I have to work harder than ever to keep my job." She sat on the edge of the couch.

"And supporting me would risk that?" He couldn't keep the bitterness out of his voice.

"He told me to stay away from the case." She sat on the edge of the couch. "If I lose that job, those benefits, I could cost my family our home. There's too much depending on me."

Which meant he shouldn't. He scrubbed his face. "Meanwhile, what about us?"

"I don't know. You said court is Thursday, so we'll know after that."

He looked at her. Was she really stalling? He wasn't a plane. He shouldn't have to circle around the airport until the storm cleared. She was worried about her job, he understood that. But at what point should he start to expect that she would be there for him?

His next suggestion seemed like a low blow, but he had to know her response. "Since the whole town knows about us, I guess we can go to town for dinner now."

A flash of panic cleared from her eyes in a heartbeat. But it'd been there. "Jesse…"

He stood. "No. I'm not going to sneak around. Look how that ended. And I'm not going to wait around for you to let everyone else decide whether I'm good enough to date or not."

"That's not fair. You know what's riding on my job."

"Your home? Have you even talked to your parents?" He didn't wait for an answer. "No, because your job is more important. Your precious reputation is more important and I'm getting in the way."

She stood, fireworks lighting the yellow flecks in her green eyes. "You expect me to throw away what I've worked hard for? I'm not the one who got sent to prison."

"Yeah, and my biggest regret with all that is that I met you." She recoiled, but his statement didn't feel like an exaggeration. "You are the best thing that's ever happened to me, but I can't keep getting shoved in the trunk. I did my time, but the city of Moore keeps thinking I should do more. The people you work with seem to think I'm unredeemable. I'm done with trying to prove myself worthy of their respect. If they can't see it, fuck 'em."

"Well, that might work for you, but it doesn't pay my bills. I worked hard to get where I'm at—"

"And you make sure we all know. Did you ever think I've worked hard to get where *I'm* at? And that I risked it for you?"

She blinked, and the line he usually found adorable creased her forehead.

Nope. She hadn't thought of it like that. It was all about her. The irony was, he'd been the selfish one in enough relationships to know the behavior when he saw it.

Storming past her, he reached the door and turned back. "I don't know what's going to happen Thursday, but if history repeats itself, I won't expect you on my visitor's roster. And if by some miracle I walk free, I'm leaving Moore. Goodbye, Farah."

He walked out. She didn't chase him. They were over. She refused to budge and he refused to be her shame. Since she clung so hard to her work, he really didn't expect to see her again. The ache in his chest at the thought only strengthened his conviction.

CHAPTER 15

Farah sat at the empty four-way stop south of town. It was Thursday and she was patrolling well away from where she lived, as well as the Walkers' area.

What had happened? Had Jesse gotten a good lawyer? Was his sister there with him?

The look on his face when he'd left... Betrayed. Hurt. Regret.

Did he regret her?

She regretted herself.

His parting words had left a mark. They'd been true. He had diligently improved himself by helping others, taking care of himself, and paying back debts he technically didn't owe. He'd used his old skills and learned a new trade he excelled at. Ranching took hard work, perseverance, and more hard work, and there were no promises that it'd work out as a profession even if all tasks were completed to perfection.

In a way, it was the opposite of her job. Both had their share of danger and unpredictability—sometimes law enforcement had more of both—and both could be mind-numbingly boring at times. But at the end of the month, she was guaranteed a paycheck at a set amount and her health insurance premiums would be paid. And if she showed up every day for twenty-nine more years, she'd receive a pension.

No such promises with ranching. It terrified her. Mom's pension had been docked when she'd had to quit before her full time was in. Dad's stress had spilled over to Farah. The two of them had battled together to regain their financial footing after Mom's stroke, but their foundation wasn't completely solid.

One thing I've learned is that when things get rough, it's easier with a good partner. I'd trade all the stability in the world over and over to spend my life with your mother.

Her talk with Dad last night had left her with thoughts. And more regrets about how she'd abandoned Jesse. His criminal past was a serious issue, but he was right. It was his past, and she kept bringing it up.

But if she didn't, her boss would. She was on notice. And now the whole town was watching the deputy who dated a criminal.

What was it Brody had said? Something about proving to everyone else he lived up to her high standards.

What about proving that she lived up to his?

After her talk with Dad, she'd written up a letter for Sheriff Allred, and she had a meeting with him in half an hour. She should call Jesse, but he didn't need the stress right now. And he might think it was a case of too little too late.

The clock clicked closer to meeting time. Should she call Jesse and see how it had gone?

No, she needed to get this task over with first. She punched her car into drive and headed toward town. Driving straight to the sheriff's office, her conviction only grew the closer she got.

She veered toward Sheriff Allred's room, nodding to the staff. A deputy showing up in the middle of a shift wasn't unusual, but she had to keep reminding herself that none of them knew why she was here.

The sheriff was at his desk, frowning into the computer. He beckoned her in.

"Did you hear the outcome?" he asked.

She didn't have to ask what he was talking about. "No. Do you know?"

"He pleaded guilty to a lesser charge and got off with a fine. The prosecutor must not have been confident he'd get him for assault."

Right. Or Jesse didn't want to stick around for a trial and had made the deal to escape Moore faster.

"But all things considered, I wouldn't flaunt your relationship around town. In fact, I think it's best if you end it before things get serious and you end up with the logistical nightmare of living under the same roof and giving a felon access to firearms."

Just a few days ago, she would've thought the same thing. But not today. "Actually, that's why I'm here." She took out her letter and handed it over. "It's my letter of resignation."

He didn't read it. Only a dark eyebrow lifted as he waited for her explanation.

"I'm not going to hide my relationship with Jesse, if I can even salvage what we had. It's not fair to him, and honestly, it's not fair to me."

"You're an officer of the law, and you're seeing—"

"I know who I'm seeing." Never in her life would she have thought she'd cut off Sheriff Allred. "I know how I met him. I also know the amazing, dependable man he's worked hard to be. I know he's taking care of himself and building a life that'd make his future niece or nephew proud to call him uncle. And I know he has my parents' seal of approval. I guess it's time to choose, and I can't work in a profession that expects me to treat one of the most important people in my life like he's nothing."

The sheriff sat back and crossed his arms. "You're quitting over a guy. I thought better of you, Deputy James."

"Think back to when you were falling for your wife. What if your boss had told you to quit seeing her in order to keep your job?"

His eyes narrowed. She might've overstepped, but she had to make a point.

"If you want a hypothetical answer to your hypothetical question," he said without inflection, "I would've thanked him for saving me the headache of my impending divorce."

Oh shit. Guess she wasn't getting a good recommendation, but then she'd been preparing to write off law enforcement altogether. She needed a career that supported her as a person, one that earned her more than a paycheck and a "watch yourself."

Impulsive decision or not, her mind was made up. "I'm sorry to hear that. This career has been my ultimate goal, but I need a life outside of my work and I hope to repair what I had with Jesse."

Her heart was racing, but she'd done it. She hadn't backed out. She just needed to find Jesse before he left town.

THE HUMIDITY WAS KILLER TODAY. Sweat trickled down Jesse's neck as he waited for Josie to pick him up. His backpack rested at his feet, packed with his few belongings. The door to Caleb's house was already locked, with Jesse's loaner key inside.

Court had gotten over nice and early. He was broke from

paying the fine, officially moved out, and stuck outside until Josie arrived.

But he was a free man. So there was that.

He thumbed through his phone to kill time. Otherwise, he'd sit and think about how peaceful the place was. Only birds, crickets, and mosquitos to disrupt the silence. If he stared at the barn, he'd think about how he'd never get to see the horses Caleb planned to purchase, never learn what a sorrel was or how to use a horse to drive cattle. Then there was the shop. Would Caleb remember to drive the pickup a couple of times a week? Jesse hadn't gotten around to servicing the snowblower. Did it even start? It was a walk-behind machine and he hadn't asked Caleb if he'd put fuel stabilizer in it and—

Yeah. He scrolled through more message boards on his phone. Waite Park had a few job openings, but Jesse seemed to have an undefined talent at finding the job that'd screw him over the most.

He looked up when Josie pulled up. The rusted green Mustang fastback purred, thanks to Josie's and Brock's mad skills. Avid collectors would probably die a slow death to see it driven on gravel, but Josie had recently acquired it and done some engine work. Once she was finished with the body, she'd sell it in a way that matched the color—for a mint. And she and Brock would probably haul it on a trailer to its happy new owner.

Wish he could be around to see it finished. But he had to save money to come back after her baby was born.

He grabbed his bag and trotted to the passenger side. Josie's look was serious. He'd confessed everything, wallowing in guilt for not telling her before half the town found out.

She was incensed on his behalf, and he was dealing with his...disappointment. That term was as weak as unleaded.

His damn heart was broken. And Farah hadn't even sent a text since he'd walked out.

For the best. His mind and his soul had a different opinion on that front, but he listened to his mind.

He wasn't a bad person. He wasn't a criminal. That was history. If he'd kept his cool enough to stay away from Clinton and Murphy, then he'd have grown out of that phase in his life. And he deserved someone who saw that, who trusted him. Someone who'd stand by him and not let him sit in jail to make herself look better.

Josie pulled away. "You sure you don't want to stay with us for a while? We have the room."

"I can't stay here. I'm the local villain no matter what I do." And he couldn't cross paths with Farah and remember how good it'd been between them. He couldn't constantly be reminded of losing the fantasy that had once been his.

"Well, if Farah ever runs for sheriff, I won't vote for her."

He settled his head back on the headrest. "Deal. How much do I owe you for the wheels?"

She huffed. "You won't want to pay a dime once you see it."

She'd found an old pickup for him and gotten it running. Jesse's expectations weren't high. It just had to carry him away from Moore.

"I'll pay you back." Eventually.

"You're paying Dillon back, but I'm family. Family does shit for each other without demanding a cut." The bitterness in her voice was directed at Bill. Her father would've found him a truck, fixed it, and then justified why Jesse owed him triple what it was worth.

"But I—"

"Jesse." Josie turned onto the highway to cross over to her side of Moore. "When I sell this thing, I'm gonna make more than most people do in a year. Don't worry about it."

That mollified him. But someday, he'd be the one giving back to people.

She turned again onto the gravel road that would take them to her place.

He peered out the window. "Those clouds are wicked."

"I guess we're in a tornado watch. I was going to tell you to look at the radar and maybe take a different route if needed."

He wasn't taking the back roads again, that was for damn sure. Had it only been two months since he'd stopped to help Caleb that day? It felt like it'd happened to a different person, except he had the heartache to prove it'd been him. "Will do" was all he said to placate Josie.

When they reached her place, he snorted a laugh. "You're kidding."

She grinned and got out, her baby bump getting more prominent, along with her glow. He rubbed his chest as he exited his side. He'd miss watching her grow. He'd have to call more often to get updates.

But part of him knew they'd slip back into their old patterns. She'd call all concerned about him and asking questions, and by the time he was done reassuring her, he'd only get the highlights of her life, not the nitty-gritty. Not that any of her life was nitty-gritty anymore, but he'd enjoyed being...well, just being her brother who lived nearby.

But being in Moore would affect her, not just him, so here he was, staring at the old truck he'd rolled that day two months ago, now refurbished.

"The body work wasn't actually that bad," she said and tossed him the keys. "When we went looking for a vehicle for you, Brock thought he'd see what happened to this one. The engine was good, the wheels..." She shrugged and put her hands behind her back to stretch. "I got all the paperwork in order. He had to do the heavy lifting on this one, but I think he liked the challenge."

Jesse feigned surprise. "What, you don't plan on selling this for a hundred and fifty grand?"

"A hundred and fifty bucks would be ambitious."

He laughed. A real one. Maybe he could do this. Live without Farah. Learn to be around people as himself without worrying what they thought of him.

He crossed to her and wrapped her in a big hug.

As she hugged him, she muttered against this shoulder, "Holy shit, what'd you do with my brother? He's usually a crabby bastard." She squeezed him in return, her belly pressing into his side.

Releasing her, he smiled. "I finally grew up."

"I, um… I thought prison would be the worst thing that could happen to you."

"I needed it." And his stay had only been long enough to scare him straight. "Weird when you wonder where I'd be if I hadn't left home and come here to break the law. I probably would've gone to work for the guy Bill was stripping parts for."

Josie nodded. "They would've set you up to take the fall if they ever got busted. And since Bill wasn't good at what he did, they would've gotten busted."

They stood next to each other and stared at the beat-up Ford. Truthfully, he probably owed Brock and Josie more time than money for this thing. But he'd take it.

The wind was picking up and clouds obscured what had been a bright sun. A storm was approaching, the promise of rain scenting the air. "I'd better get going. It's pretty blue on the horizon."

"I don't like the green tinge to it. Why don't you stay here until the storm passes?"

Intuition prodded at him to hit the road. If he stayed with

Josie to wait out the bad weather, then it'd be late and he'd stay for supper. Then he'd stay overnight and tomorrow might bring another excuse to stick around Moore. And he'd already proven that his presence here wasn't good for those he cared about the most.

"I'll take the highway." No shortcut today. It'd take him too close to Farah's property, and from the looks of it, right into the deepest of the blue. He gave the clouds one last look. Josie was right. There was an odd yellow to the horizon that gave it an overall green tinge.

That was an ugly storm. "You're going inside as soon as I leave, right?"

Her hair was getting kicked around by the wind. It'd gotten even stronger while they were standing here.

"Yes, and Brock will be home any minute to wait it out with me. Go." She gave him another quick hug.

He hopped in. The smell of old upholstery and faint oil was familiar, almost welcome. This pickup was his. They were both survivors. He'd pay back his sister, but now he had a backpack and wheels. See? Things were improving.

ood God, that was an ugly picture. He slowed on the highway and pulled to the right. Traffic was nonexistent, like everyone else knew better than to be out in the open when the sky looked like a green-gray menace. He rolled to a stop and pulled out his phone.

A message from Farah. *Can we talk?*

Hope surged. She'd texted! But no. He was done talking. If he talked to Farah, he might linger in Moore and what was the saying? That way lay insanity?

Instead, he opened his weather app. It sat on the opening page, struggling to download in the middle of nowhere with spotty reception.

Dammit. He flipped on the radio. Florida Georgia Line crooned through the speakers. No severe weather warning interrupted the song. It must look worse than it was.

Why did he care? He was driving away from it. The storm would pass over Moore and keep heading east until it faded out. He'd go northwest and then cut east. He might experience rain at the most.

But those clouds were getting closer where he'd just come

from.

Clenching his jaw, he put the pickup in gear. As he was accelerating, electronic beeps cut through the radio. He pulled to the side again and listened, his stomach sinking with each word.

The watch was now a warning. Didn't that mean a funnel cloud had been spotted?

Hail. Damaging winds. Heavy rain. Seek shelter.

He was worried about Josie, but she had a solid basement and Brock was with her.

Farah. Fuck, she'd be out in this.

She wasn't his to worry about anymore. Didn't mean he could quit. Did she have to be out on the roads? Could she find shelter in time?

Caleb was working. He'd probably be in a similar boat as Farah but out in the aftermath.

Maybe it'd be only rain. Anyway, the people he cared about could take care of themselves.

He eased off the brake, then slammed it again.

What about Farah's parents?

Corinne couldn't do stairs. He looked at the sky. Lightning cut across clouds.

A few seconds later, thunder cracked across the land.

The Jameses were probably downstairs. He let off the brake.

Only to stomp on it again.

What if they weren't? What if Derrick was busy securing all the windows and doors and getting vehicles inside?

Jesse peered over his shoulder and cranked the wheel to the side. Laying on the accelerator, he peeled out, leaving a strip of black on the pavement. The squeal of his tires was lost in the thunder.

He plowed through the shallow median to the other side of the highway and gunned it.

The engine roared. Dust and debris were getting kicked up, blowing across the road, his truck rocking with the wind.

Fat raindrops splattered his windshield, but it wasn't the deluge he'd expected.

He drove, leaning over the wheel to monitor the sky. Smaller clouds roamed underneath the dark canopy. Each time he spotted one, he worried it could be a funnel cloud.

Slowing only to take the turn that'd bring him to the Jameses, he took his eyes off the road. His gut twisted.

He was driving into the damn heart of the storm, toward people who may already be hunkered down.

But the stairs. Corinne couldn't do stairs, and Farah said she was slow. What if Corinne fell in her rush?

The dust from Jesse's tires was blown away with the rest of the grit hitting the pickup.

How he didn't skid off the road and crash, he didn't know, but he reached the Jameses blue house.

The green tint to the clouds left him with a sick feeling, and the low-hanging clouds had more suspicious projections sticking out of them. He didn't know if they were wisps of rain or if a tornado would land on his head, but his brain was screaming at him to get inside.

He slammed to a stop by the house, changed his mind, and moved his truck farther away. Grabbing the door handle, he paused. A whoosh of wind pelted the pickup, shaking it like a can of pop.

How long did he wait it out?

Fuck it. He pushed the door open, needing to give it an extra shove with his shoulder. It slammed shut behind him as he sprinted toward the house.

Suddenly the wind died down. The world around him was quiet. Not even a bird dared to tweet. But the green in the sky had deepened.

His heart slammed against his ribs. This was the literal

calm before the storm.

He banged the Jameses' door open. "Derrick! You guys okay?"

"Jesse?" Derrick's voice was muffled.

Jesse ran into the living room, but there was only the staircase going up.

"Derrick?" Where the hell were the stairs to the basement? He'd never been down there.

"Get down here, son!"

Jesse followed the voice through the kitchen and around a corner. He'd never been in this part of the house. A wooden door.

He opened it, the door acting more like a locked full steel door than a hollow-core interior door. His ears started to pop. The air pressure was changing. He braced himself and shoved with his shoulder. Derrick was two stairs below Corinne, helping her take one stair at a time.

A loud rumble filled the air, and his hearing went muffled like his ears were filled with fluid. Derrick's wide eyes met Jesse's, then shifted to the door.

Corrine was probably the calmest out of all of them. She tensed but continued to tackle the next stair.

"I apologize in advance." Jesse rushed down to her. There was barely enough room in the stairwell for them to be shoulder to shoulder. He waved Derrick down and swung Corrine into his arms.

She squeaked, but released the railing and clung to his shirt. The walls vibrated. It was like a freight train was charging right over the house.

Derrick was already at the bottom of the stairs, pointing around the corner. Jesse didn't question him. He held Corinne and rushed to the opening under the stairs. Boxes of empty canning jars clogged the lowest parts, but there was enough room for all three of them.

Jesse lowered Corrine all the way to the bare concrete floor in the corner of the room. He crouched on one side of her and Derrick kneeled on the other. What good they'd do for her if the house collapsed on top of them, he didn't know, but old-school drills ran through his mind. Get low. Cover your head.

His shoulder was butted up against the cool foundation where no wainscoting had been hung. The concrete trembled. Corrine's hands were above her head, Derrick and James a solid wall of fleshy protection.

Now all they could do was wait.

"Seriously." Farah kept an eye on the sky as she pulled up behind the black pickup on the side of the highway.

Daniel was putting his spare on, but unless he set a speed record in tire changing, he was going to get caught in the storm.

She didn't even bother to get out. As she stopped, she glanced at her phone. Last her dad texted, he was battening down the hatches. She'd told him to get downstairs. Warnings were going off all over the place, and living in the country where there were no tornado sirens, they had to police themselves.

He hadn't gotten back to her. Were they downstairs? Had he gotten Mom down okay?

She glared at the black pickup. The one she suspected had run Jesse off the road.

Had Jesse left already and missed the bad weather? She wouldn't know. He hadn't returned her message.

Yes, he had to have. Why would he stay?

She ground her teeth and opened the window. A flurry of dust and dirt whirled inside. Blinking and spitting grit out of her mouth, she shouted, "Daniel!"

He didn't so much as glance at her but kept cranking at the lug nuts. She was blocking half the damn road, but everyone else had enough sense to be off it. They were two miles away from his property. He must've been racing the storm home like she'd been when his tire had blown. The replacement rested against the truck's frame. He hadn't even gotten the old one off yet. There was no time.

"Daniel! Get in here."

He finally glanced up from where he was kneeling by his rear driver's side wheel, his wide eyes wild, his mouth opening from his frantic panting. The guy was scared. She didn't like him, but she didn't want to see him battered to death from the storm, or sizzling from a strike of lightning.

"Get in," she ordered.

He took one last look at the sky and rose, hobbling to the door. Good, he was listening.

He dove into the passenger seat. "Go."

To where? They should head away from the worst of it, but they needed to seek shelter. His house was closer. She could take the turn a couple miles before her normal one and take a few back roads. Sheltering down with the Bradford brothers wasn't her ideal situation, but neither was getting flung across Moore like she was Dorothy going to Oz.

She sped toward Clinton's, radioing in to dispatch where she was heading and who she had with her. The wind was brutal. At least there was no hail. Some lightning tore across the sky, but at least it wasn't aimed toward the ground. A grass fire was the last thing she needed in this weather.

"Is your brother home?" she asked. She had to make sure he wasn't out checking cattle or tampering with Caleb's land. Her oath to protect citizens included even those she couldn't stand the sight of.

"Yes. He called me and told me to get home as he was

heading downstairs." Daniel hugged his arms around himself. An inkling of empathy snaked in. Deep down, Daniel wasn't a bad guy, just led astray by his brutish brother. Clinton had gotten the looks and charisma and Daniel had been his faithful admirer.

Their farm approached. She drove by here often, both for her job and as an excuse to see if they were up to anything, and each time she had to stop and marvel at how much nicer it was. Bigger, more spread out. He had a pole barn, a picturesque red barn, a Morton shop, and the house. Their parents had built it before they'd handed the reins over to the boys. A rambling ranch with a log cabin look. The place could be used for postcards of Minnesota farm life.

But as nice as it was, this whole area was in the same danger from the storm.

The car shook with the wind as she pulled into the drive. Daniel pointed to an open door in the barn. "Clint left it open for my truck. Pull inside. There's an old cellar entrance on the outside."

Outside was the last place any of them wanted to be.

She pulled inside, slammed on the brakes, and cut the engine. They both rolled out and ran for the exit. She had no idea where this cellar was, but they needed to get there.

Daniel stopped to pull the door shut. The wind died. Sudden silence descended.

They both stopped to look around. Daniel's face filled with determination as he tackled sliding the door closed.

"No time!" Farah grabbed his arm and yanked him away. "Where's the cellar?" Her ears filled with pressure.

Shit.

A roar started building, way too close.

Daniel's face drained of all color and he stumbled as he tried to turn back. "The door."

"The cellar," she yelled over the noise and doubled down on towing him away.

Finally, his mind switched gears and he ran ahead of her. She didn't let go of him.

Old, faded wooden doors a foot above the ground were next to the wall. She helped Daniel wrestle one heavy flank open. She shoved him down first, hoping he didn't trip on the rickety stairs. The cellar was original and hadn't been updated with the barn.

Musty earth surrounded her as she descended after Daniel. She lowered the door above her. If there was a way to secure it, she didn't know and there was no time to check. They crowded into a damp corner. Antique metal creamery jugs made a good base to crouch on, and she had zero qualms about bugs and grime.

The noise was like being under the hood of an eighteen-wheeler.

She wanted to push her hands against her popping ears, but Daniel was shaking so bad, she had to monitor him. The guy looked on the brink of a heart attack. He rocked back and forth, his arms thrown over his head. The doors vibrated, occasionally flipping up and ramming back against the frame. Both she and Daniel flinched each time. The earth trembled and vibrated around them.

She tapped on his knee. "Inhaler?"

"P-pocket."

Good. She only had to worry about his heart, not his lungs.

As they waited out the storm and worried their old shelter wouldn't hold, Farah had so many regrets. At least one of her regrets should be far enough away from this storm to be safe. The world was getting ripped apart around them, but hers had been ruined as soon as she'd let him down.

CHAPTER 17

The drone of the storm faded.

"Oh my God," Corrine mumbled. "Is it over?"

Derrick shook his head, but his whole body was shaking. Jesse probably looked the same. He straightened, his muscles protesting after being clamped down in survival so long.

Derrick groaned as he stood. "It sounded like the tornado went right over us, but I think the house is at least standing."

"Is it safe to go back upstairs?" Jesse asked. He wanted to rush out and check the damage, but he had to help Corrine.

"I think so." Derrick glanced down at his wife like he was trying to solve the puzzle of how to get her back upstairs.

"Where's Farah?" She'd been on his mind the whole time. What was Farah doing? Had she gotten someplace safe?

"I'll—I'll call her." Derrick pulled his phone out. "Let's hope the cell tower wasn't destroyed."

They waited in tense silence as he tried dialing.

"Shit," Jesse growled, too afraid to be horrified about swearing around the Jameses.

"She found a spot." Corrine dipped her head in a way

none of them could argue with. She knew her daughter and she knew the job.

Jesse stooped and swung Corrine up into his arms once more.

"Damn." Derrick's voice grew thick. "I'm glad you stopped by."

Jesse didn't answer. He had to see how bad the damage was. What had been destroyed. Who.

He charged up the stairs and was about to wrestle the door open when Derrick wedged his hand from behind to turn the knob. The door swung open. Jesse cautiously stepped out.

Frames had been knocked to the floor. The place was quiet. No power.

But the house was standing. He settled Corrine on her feet. She patted his shoulder and he darted outside.

Tree branches littered the yard along with scraps of wood and bits of green shingles. A couple of the oldest trees in the tree rows had been felled and some branches were shredded from the wind.

Horror dawned on him. The James place was an oasis. But if he looked toward the road, it was like a dozer had taken a path across the field. The damage was worse beyond the trees, toward Caleb's.

He sprinted to the path he usually took, but it was clogged with downed branches and debris. Jesse spun around. Where'd all the debris come from?

The James house had seen better days, but other than damaged Masonite siding and missing shingles, it was sturdy. The shop was fine. The barn. Derrick would have to deal with the horses. Jesse would help check cattle later.

He sprinted down the driveway, jumping over random objects scattered over the ground. A large branch the size of his leg, a splintered two by four, and what looked to be muddled fabric. Oh hell, if the James house and all their buildings were standing, where'd the fabric come from?

Running past the trees, he cut through the ditch. More debris scattered the ground. Clothing was stuck in trees, stark against the stripped limbs. He slowed at one large piece of fabric hanging in the trees like a limp flag.

The quilt Caleb's grandma had made. Jesse tore down the lane and gasped, sliding to a stop. His eyes were wide, his chest heaving from the run. The devastation was unbelievable. Caleb's house had been demolished. It was like a giant had picked it up and crunched it in his fist and shaken the bits to the ground.

"Oh my God." Jesse's heart broke for his friend.

Caleb had dedicated his life to reinvigorating that ranch and now he didn't even have a home. The garage and barn were leveled. Jesse couldn't distinguish the specific path of the tornado, but the shop and barn had gotten the worst. Even the riding lawn mower was gone. The house had been on the outer edge. Collateral damage.

He craned his neck around. The field behind him was torn up and he couldn't see beyond that. Murphy's house was a mile away and north and east of the land he farmed. Jesse jogged back out to the road. The trail of ripped-up land originated away from Murphy's. Good. If there was only one tornado, and this was where it had hit, then Josie should be safe. And there'd be no reason for Farah to have been in the area when the storm hit.

He pulled out his phone. No signal. Dammit.

Jesse peered down the road. Fence was twisted and, in several sections, missing entirely. The cattle!

He tensed to run to the pasture, but relaxed. Caleb's four-wheeler was buried and he'd likely get stuck on a pile of tornado droppings. With no veterinary skills and no way to transport those that were injured, Jesse was useless for the cows. And he had to see if any of the other neighbors had been hit.

It all depended on how long the tornado had touched down. Caleb's and the Jameses' south pastures were behind the house. Then it was the Bradfords' property. Jesse had never seen their house, only the copse of trees surrounding Clinton's house. Jesse would have to check. Clinton was the closest neighbor and most likely to be in the path of the tornado.

Fuck. Jesse started running.

His lungs burned and his legs were tired. When he'd first arrived in Moore, if he'd had to run cross-country while dodging obstacles, he'd have been toast in seconds. But working outside all day and push mowing that damn lawn of Caleb's had provided a better level of conditioning.

Once he'd reached Clinton's land, where there was no longer any fence to impede his run, Jesse was still passing bits of Caleb's house and barn. None of it was recognizable, only bits of color from the siding and barn.

His hopes sank further the closer he got to Clinton's. The trees around the house hadn't fared as well as the ones around the Jameses'. Entire trees had been ripped out of the ground. Some were toppled with their enormous root balls wrenched out of the ground. The amount of debris increased the closer Jesse got, and he couldn't make out any roofs beyond the trees.

He might not like Clinton or Daniel, but he couldn't just turn his back and ignore them.

Veering off his path, he had to slow down to pick and choose where to step in order to get to the yard. He found an area of the trees that was sparser than the rest. Picking his way through, gnarled branches snagged his shirt, tearing it in a few places, but he reached the clearing on the other side. Clinton's property was the opposite of Caleb's. The house had taken the worst while the outbuildings had been clipped. The huge metal shop was still standing but covered in dents so large it was like someone had tossed small vehicles into the sides.

Grain bins were twisted and two were missing their tops altogether. The barn hadn't withstood the force, but it hadn't been ripped apart like the house.

A yell caught his attention. It sounded like a man's. Was only one brother home?

"Where are you?" Jesse yelled.

"Here," came the faint reply. "Daniel?"

Jesse ran to the house. He hadn't felt so useless in his whole damn life. All those other times, he'd been figuratively useless, more melancholy than truly worthless. Now, he couldn't lift a damn house off a man. He had nothing more than a phone with no cell reception. Unless he needed the calculator app, it was fucking worthless.

"Clinton?" Jesse stepped through the debris, inspecting what was in front of him before he put each foot down. He couldn't remember a damn thing about storms and downed power lines, only not to touch them.

"Daniel? Oh God, I'm here."

"No, I'm not Daniel. Where are you?" Jesse hollered.

Silence. Then, "Where's—where's Daniel? Who are you?"

Clinton was close. And he was under the heap of boards, collapsed walls, and toppled furniture. Jesse couldn't get close enough to see him, but he could at least make sure Clinton would survive where he was. He might have to circle around to the other side and see if he could reach Clinton from there.

"Jesse. Caleb's hired hand. Where are you? Are you hurt?"

"Do you see Daniel?"

That answered none of Jesse's questions, but he couldn't

blame the guy. He was worried about his brother. Daniel was probably doing better than the rest of them.

"I saw them drive up, but the tornado hit and I couldn't get outside. Where are they?" Panic was filling Clinton's voice.

They? "Who?"

"Daniel!" Clinton was either yelling louder or had positioned himself by an opening in the remnant of his house. "He got a flat and Farah gave him a ride."

Jesse's heart slammed to a stop. Farah had been here? She'd been here when the tornado had hit? "Where are they?" Jesse yelled, spinning around. Oh God. The destruction.

"You can't see them?" A sob wrenched from Clinton. "Daniel! Daniel!"

"Shut up!" Jesse wasn't heartless, but he couldn't look or listen with Clinton shouting. "They didn't make it to the house?"

"No. God, can you find him? Please find Daniel. I promised Mom I'd look out for him."

Farah was here and missing. Daniel was missing. Clinton was able to talk so he should be fine. As much as a guy could be with a house sitting on him. But both he and Clinton seemed to agree that finding their missing loved ones was more important.

"Where could they be?" Please let there be someplace underground besides the basement. But as Jesse scanned the property, his hopes sank. No barn or shop he'd ever heard of had a basement.

"Cellar. By the barn."

Fuck, yeah. Jesse spun, wobbling to keep his balance and not fall. Too many bared nails waiting to impale him.

Clinton had said the barn. There were two metal buildings. One was a pole barn. Had he meant that or the straight-up barn? Or the small square building behind the shop that looked oddly untouched? No, that'd be more of a shed.

Thank God living with Caleb had tutored him on all things outbuilding. Jesse chose the standard barn first. It was the oldest building and the one most likely to have something like a cellar.

"Farah!" he called as he picked his way over. "Daniel!" He stopped to listen.

"Daniel!" That was from Clinton. His yell told Jesse the man was still alive, but Clinton needed to be quiet.

He peered into the scattered wood of the barn. Half of it was still standing. Like the grain bins, its roof was gone. Two walls had tipped in. It looked the main door had been open. He crouched to peer inside. "Farah?"

Was that white paint? Oh no. It was her patrol car. His absurd fantasy that Clinton had been hallucinating died a harsh death.

"Farah! Daniel!" He strained to listen, but sirens in the distance interfered. Of all the times for help to arrive. Would they come here first, or had Derrick been able to reach them somehow?

He made it to one side of the barn but found nothing that'd indicate a cellar entrance. What if the entrance was inside?

He didn't know a damn thing about cellars! But he was outside. He might as well check both sides before crawling in. Because if Farah was in that building, he'd tear it down with his bare hands to get to her.

The sun was shining, almost like an apology for the storm that had passed, and Jesse was grateful for the light.

"Farah! Daniel!"

He'd made it to the other side and found the roof. For all his boasts of tearing the place down— What was he going to do?

"Farah!"

"Jesse?" Farah's muffled voice made him want to drop to his knees.

"Farah! Is Daniel with you?"

"Yes, but he's not doing well."

Jesse thought for a second about turning back to shout to Clinton that he'd found them, but it was too urgent. Daniel was in trouble and Farah was buried. He didn't want to leave for any reason and he didn't want to delay.

A scrape of wood resonated from under the pile of green barn shingles. Maybe if he dropped to his stomach and wedged under the debris…? Something was holding it off the ground.

He tossed a few boards to the side. Most of the pieces were small. The roof rested against the barn like it'd been lifted and shoved off the side. But had it made it a tent over the cellar entrance?

Dropping to his belly, he wiggled underneath.

Dirt and old-barn mustiness assaulted his nose and he couldn't see a damn thing.

He wiggled as close as he could and pulled out his phone. Before he could get the flashlight on, a beam shone into his face.

"Jesse. What are you doing?"

"Coming to help." He squinted against Farah's flashlight—the only heat he cared about her packing. He glanced around the tight spot. The pile of weathered timber on top of the cellar doors would prevent them from being opened more than a foot.

"It could collapse on you. I was able to get through to dispatch. The fire department should be on their way."

He was intensely grateful for the gear she had to wear. Her dusty face peeked out of a crack in the doors and she swept the light around the cramped space.

"Oh my God, the whole barn came down on top of us." Her breath hitched. "My parents."

"They're fine. We got downstairs in time. Caleb's place is gone."

A low keen emanated from behind her. The wailing grew louder and she shone the light down into the cellar.

"I think he's going to put himself into shock," she hissed. "He was hyperventilating and he's been incoherent for the last few minutes. I gotta get him out of here."

Jesse nodded, but he doubted Farah could see. "Daniel? I talked to Clinton before I got here. He made it through the storm." The cry turned into a whimper. "Can you take a deep breath? Let it out slowly?"

He met Farah's gaze. She pushed on the door and it opened another inch. They only needed it open far enough to wedge themselves out.

He had no idea if Daniel was listening to him, but if he could distract the guy enough to keep him from being a medical emergency, Farah could use the time to figure a way out.

Where was the fire department? Their sirens had died down, or Jesse just couldn't hear them with half a barn over his head.

"Take a breath in, Daniel." Jesse counted to five. "Now let it out and repeat, 'I am calm. I am collected. I am in control.'" He continued to repeat the words himself, stopping only when footsteps crunched behind him.

"Who's in there? Jesse?" Caleb's voice rang out.

Jesse craned his head around to look behind him. Beyond his feet were black boots and the thick pants firemen wore. "It's me. Farah and Daniel are in the cellar. Clinton's in the basement of the house. The Jameses are okay."

"Shit. You've been busy. Listen, we can't get the truck

through here without stranding ourselves. The county's getting their heavy equipment out here."

More boots shuffled on the gravel. Caleb's voice drifted in as he updated his coworkers.

"Farah?" It took a moment for Jesse to place Max's voice. "Are either one of you hurt?"

Farah's head popped back out. "No, but Daniel's going to need medical attention. How's Clinton?"

Max crouched down and peered at them, swearing when he saw the tight space and buried door. "I can't get through to him. He's too worried about Daniel. Can you get him out of there?"

"I can help pry the door open," Jesse offered.

"We need to brace this," Caleb said and his boots disappeared.

Jesse wiggled as close to Farah as he could. Lights flashed all over as Max and the other firefighters discussed how they could make the structure as safe as possible to get them out.

"Daniel," Jesse called. "Are you still doing your breathing?"

"I'm sorry," Daniel sobbed.

"He confessed to everything," Farah said quietly. "The fence, the cattle, the pictures. Leaving the scene of your accident. Even Dillon's fire."

Jesse thought he'd be happier, but their problems were so much bigger now. Safety was the priority now. None of them were turning away from this mission over personal reasons.

"Do you think we can get him out of there?" he asked.

Farah visually measured the foot-wide opening she'd managed to coax at one end and scanned the distance to where Max and the firemen were working at the edge of the pile. Jesse shifted, a flash of pain searing his shoulder. He must've gotten too high and hit an exposed nail. Good thing he was up to date on his tetanus shot.

"We'll have to get this open a little more, but yeah. It's

doable. I just don't know if we'll unsettle the mess and bury ourselves worse."

"We get him out and Max and Caleb can drag him past the debris. We'll worry about the rest after." Farah should be safe in the cellar. It wasn't airtight and those doors were solid. Jesse wasn't worried about himself.

"Caleb?" Jesse called over his shoulder.

"Yeah, man."

"We think we can get Daniel out and he can do the snake to you."

Caleb had dropped to his knees and was peering at him. With all the flashlights shining through the pile of rubble, Jesse could make out dusty faces and tense expressions. "We'll grab him as soon as he's close. Be careful."

"I'll go get him." Farah ducked down, the door shut on top of her. Jesse's heart crawled into his throat every time she disappeared from view.

The door budged open again. Wide, terrified eyes peeked out.

"Clinton can't wait to hear from you," Jesse said.

Daniel's gaze caught his. He nodded. "He's okay?"

"I don't know," Jesse answered honestly. "He's too worried about you to tell us how he's doing."

Daniel dragged in a ragged breath, but the high-pitched whine on the end of his exhale was a new development. He was wheezing and it was getting worse. "Okay. What do I do?" Yeah, he sounded out of breath.

"Crawl out, but stay as low as you can and come toward me. The way out is right behind me and they're waiting for you."

Daniel nodded, looked around, and then wedged his head out. He grunted, coughed, and pushed a shoulder through.

There wasn't going to be enough room. Jesse had tackled him that day. The guy was bigger than him and it didn't matter if it was fat, muscle, or a beer gut, Daniel needed a wider opening.

Jesse slithered to the low base of the cellar door. The worst of the pressure on the doors was near the top that arched upward into the side of the barn. Just two more inches.

"What's wrong?" Farah called from below.

"He needs more room," Jesse grunted as he wedged himself to his knees, pressing his shoulders upward, shifting to find a place where he wasn't jabbed by nails.

"I think I…" Daniel coughed again, but he didn't quit wiggling.

Jesse huffed out a breath and strained up. He couldn't lift half a building, but all he needed was a few centimeters.

Daniel's other shoulder popped free. He was grunting and coughing, but he didn't stop.

Farah encouraged him from below. Daniel didn't stop and Caleb's voice chimed in.

Wood groaning made them all pause. The pile of rubble was shifting.

"Hurry," Jesse panted. He wedged a leg out. Daniel would have to crawl under it on his way out, but Jesse needed the leverage.

His muscles protested, jagged wood cutting into his shoulders. He wished he could lend Daniel a hand and yank him out, but Jesse needed four points of contact to keep the barn roof off of them.

"This isn't stable," Caleb shouted. "Daniel, go back in. Jesse, can you get in with them? You'll all be protected—"

The idea must've driven a spike of fear into Daniel, because he shot out of the opening with an oomph. Wheezing and coughing, he army crawled close enough to Caleb.

Wood creaked and it was like someone had dumped a few

hundred pounds onto Jesse's shoulder. His boot was slipping and his mind was racing through scenarios. Farah was safe in the cellar. He could drop to the ground by the doors and pray nothing was long enough to impale him.

But as soon as Daniel's legs disappeared into the sunlight, two hands grabbed Jesse's shirt and pulled. He tumbled through the door, adjusting enough to put his head and arms in first. The cacophony of shifting debris was deafening as he crashed to the ground inside the cellar.

THE BREATH WAS KNOCKED out of Farah as Jesse landed on top of her. The door slammed shut and chunks of wood echoed through the cellar as they rained down on the closed entrance.

But Jesse was safe.

He groaned and lifted to his hands and knees. Stickiness coated her fingers where she'd hugged him to her as they fell down the rickety stairs.

"You're bleeding." She pushed him up to his knees and got to her own to do a quick inspection. He was grimy, his black T-shirt was in tatters, and his jeans were ripped, but he looked amazing. She angled her light to his back. The blood originated from a few small wounds. She couldn't find anything severe.

"A nail got me. Pretty tame, considering."

Nodding, she dropped the light, clasped both sides of his face, and kissed him hard. Distant shouting was the only thing that made her stop.

She leaned back to shout, "We're fine."

Her radio crackled and Max's voice came through. "You two alive?"

"We're safe. Take your time. Get Clinton to safety. Even if

the doors don't hold, half this cellar is dug underground and away from the doors. We're fine."

"Roger. Check in every five minutes until my damn heart rate settles down."

"Got it, Max." She took her finger off the button and met Jesse's dark gaze. The light from her flashlight was bouncing off the walls, casting sinister shadows over his face. Her belly flipped.

So sexy.

"Keep looking at me like that and I might see how far you want to carry that kiss."

"All the way." She threw her arms around him. "I can't believe you're here."

His arms wound around her. She was back in his embrace and hoping Max and the fire department took a few hours.

"I'd say I can't believe you're here, but it's kind of your job," he murmured into her hair.

"I found Daniel with a flat and the sky was telling me we would be stupid to stay out there. We barely made it down here in time."

They settled on the floor away from the doors. His back was against the musty boards that made up the flimsy wall built against the dirt. She cuddled under his arm as much as her vest would allow.

"Is Caleb's place really destroyed?" How awful. He'd tried so hard to save that place.

"Demolished. I don't think he'll be able to rescue any of the buildings. Maybe he can recover some small items, but all his belongings are in the fields and pastures. I didn't want to tell him that while he's here trying to save people. But it's…sad."

"Yeah. Mom and Dad, how…"

"I was leaving town and planned to go around the weather, but then I thought of your mom's trouble with stairs and what if she and your dad didn't get started down-stairs right away."

"You're a good guy, Jesse."

He didn't say anything, and he didn't look at her. Because he knew he was a good guy. Only she hadn't shown him that she knew.

"I quit my job today."

"What?" He dropped his arm and twisted to look at her. They were even farther from where she'd left her light. She should get it, but staying close to him was more important.

"I shouldn't have to choose. And any workplace and coworkers who don't trust me to know what's best for my personal life can suck it." The emptiness welled. Her work had become her identity. What would she do now?

Figure out who Farah James really was.

"You— But you're— Why?"

"Because, Jesse Rodriguez, I fell in love with you and they told me I was wrong. I dedicated my life to them and they couldn't give you five minutes."

"I was arrested when they found out we were dating." He shrugged, his hand shooting up to his wounded shoulder.

"Because Daniel and Clinton wanted to be assholes." She rolled to her knees again and put her hands on his shoulders. "I know you have a past, and the business with Daniel looked bad, but that's all they saw. I thought they knew me. They should have known I wouldn't lose my shit over a guy." She smiled. "Well, not just any guy. I told Sheriff Allred as much and gave him my letter. I may have used an analogy that involved his wife."

"I can't imagine that went over well."

"I won't lie, I thought I'd get canned on the spot. He's going through a divorce."

He stared at her. "I can't believe you quit."

"I was going to finish my shift and chase you down. I gave them two weeks' notice, but I'm off tomorrow."

He tugged her closer. "Did you say you fell in love with me?"

She rested her forehead against his. "Yep."

"I have no job. No place to live." A wry smile lit his face. "But Brock resurrected that Ford I showed up in town with."

She traced the side of his face. "I happen to have a place to live, but no job."

"I guess we'll have to figure it out together. Because I love you, too."

She repressed a triumphant smile. Instead she depressed her radio button and spoke into it. "1506 checking in."

Max's voice came back. "Got it, 1506."

Settling over Jesse's lap, she stripped off her vest off and rested it against the wall. "We have five minutes. Whatever are we going to do?"

CHAPTER 18

Sweat trickled between his shoulder blades. September in Minnesota shouldn't be so hot. Jesse wiped the sweat off his brow as he rode Petunia in the ditch to inspect the fence line. Much of it'd had to be replaced after the tornado. The Jameses had teamed up with Caleb and his best friend Justin and they'd gotten it done. Caleb was staying at Justin's house and the Jameses were letting him use their place as home base for his small eighty-head cattle operation.

Jesse and Derrick ranched both herds to give Caleb breathing room while he cleaned up his property, dealt with insurance, and planned the rebuild. Jesse was no longer Caleb's hired hand—his friend needed to save his money— but that didn't mean Jesse was abandoning him. They'd recovered and accounted for all the cattle. Not one had been lost, and none had wandered, instinctively staying in a low area and away from flying debris.

Jesse pulled in a deep breath. Between cleanup efforts, riding horse, and fishing, he had plenty of outlets for any pent-up emotions. He was freer than he'd been in his whole life. And he had a home.

He'd moved in with Farah almost right away, and her parents loved having him around. There was still the issue of his access to her firearms, but they'd scraped together some cash for a gun safe. He didn't have the code for it and therefore technically didn't have access. Sure, it was a gray area, but it was a chance both of them were willing to take.

He heard the engine before a white patrol car pulled up on the road next to him.

Farah rolled the window down. "Do you have a license for that thing?"

He laughed. Every day he rode, enjoying the noise a horse made over the sound of a four-wheeler. Something he'd thought his mechanic heart would never prefer. "Your mom cleared my credentials before I took her out. Done with work?"

After they'd been rescued from the cellar—not that he'd been in any rush to finish their heavy make-out session—the sheriff had returned her resignation. He'd said he hadn't planned on letting a good deputy like her go, but after what Jesse had done during the storm, the sheriff didn't anticipate any issues. Of course, his tone had also said, *as long as you don't fuck up*, which Jesse didn't plan on doing.

"Yes. Are you heading home?" Home. He never got tired of asking her that. Nowhere else had felt so much like home than her shop apartment.

She nodded. "Clinton's insurance cleared and he delivered a check to the office. One each for me, you, and Caleb to pay for the truck, the cows he stole, and the fence he destroyed. And your check also includes the thousand dollars you were fined because of Daniel."

The men were trying to reform, and Jesse believed that it would last. Family was a powerful motivator.

Once Clinton had been pulled from the remains of his house with a shallow head wound and a dislocated shoulder from trying to escape, he'd only been focused on Daniel's safety. As well as humbled and grateful for Farah and Jesse's role in Daniel's rescue, considering what they'd done. Farah and Jesse were Daniel's heroes now and that gave him equal footing with the brother he'd idolized.

With the aftermath of the storm to concentrate on and the threat of losing their livelihood and their property, the brothers had agreed to reimburse Farah and Caleb for damages done, in return for not pursuing legal action. They were neighbors now, nothing more but nothing less.

He whistled. Petunia's ears swiveled, but she stood still. "What are we going to do with all that money?"

Farah grinned. They both knew it wasn't a lot, and all but his truck and fine reimbursement would get put back into the ranch. He'd pay Josie back for his beater pickup. It was still running, so he wasn't in a hurry to car shop. And he had his regular payment to Dillon to make.

But he had to pretend that he had no other plans for the remainder. Because as soon as the check was deposited and Farah went to work again, he was going to buy a ring. A simple gold band. Farah wouldn't want a fancier one. It'd get in the way of ranching and patrolling. He'd picked it out already.

"I thought we could go out tonight," Farah said. "It's two-for-one-burger night at Tyler's and the guys from work are getting together."

His stomach growled in response. He made good use of her grill, but some days it was nice to not have to do the cooking.

"Why, Deputy James, are you asking me out on a date?" They'd only been out twice since the storm. Between working overtime from the aftermath and funneling money into their place for repairs, not to mention helping Caleb where possible, going out to eat was a luxury.

"You *are* my person of interest," she joked. "See you in a bit."

She pulled away and he turned Petunia around. By the time Farah greeted her parents and went inside to clean up, he'd get back, brush down Petunia, turn her out into the pasture, and join Farah in the shower.

When he'd first come to Moore, he'd thought he'd lost it all—and that the people in this town had taken the rest. But Moore had given him everything back, and more besides. A home, a family, and now a future.

WILL Caleb ever get a chance to defrost Brigit's icy exterior in Red Hot Rancher?

FOR AN EXTRA EPILOGUE, sign up for my newsletter and also get all the latest news, sneak peeks, quarterly short stories, and bonus material.

I'D LOVE to hear what you thought. You can drop a quick review of Rancher in Training at the retailer.

ABOUT THE AUTHOR

Marie Johnston writes paranormal and contemporary romance and has collected several awards in both genres. Before she was a writer, she was a microbiologist. Depending on the situation, she can be oddly unconcerned about germs or weirdly phobic. She's also a licensed medical technician and has worked as a public health microbiologist and as a lab tech in hospital and clinic labs. Marie's been a volunteer EMT, a college instructor, a security guard, a phlebotomist, a hotel clerk, and a coffee pourer in a bingo hall. All fodder for a writer!! She has four kids, an old cat, and a puppy that's bigger than half her kids.

mariejohnstonwriter.com
Facebook
Twitter @mjohnstonwriter

Part-Time Cowboys

Rancher in Training (Book 1)

Red Hot Rancher (Book 2)

White Collar Rancher (Book 3)

Rancher Next Door (Book 4)

Her Christmas Offer (novella)

The Walker Five:

Conflict of Interest (Book 1)

Mustang Summer (Book 2)

Long Hard Fall (Book 3)

Guilt Ridden (Book 4)

Mail Order Farmer (Book 5)

9 781951 067052